Open Water

Open Water

CALEB AZUMAH NELSON

VIKING

an imprint of

PENGUIN BOOKS

VIKING

UK | USA | Canada | Ireland | Australia
India | New Zealand | South Africa

Viking is part of the Penguin Random House group of companies
whose addresses can be found at global.penguinrandomhouse.com

First published 2021
003

Set in 11/13 pt Dante MT Std
Typeset by Jouve (UK), Milton Keynes
Printed and bound in Great Britain by Clays Ltd, Elcograf S.p.A.

The authorized representative in the EEA is Penguin Random House Ireland,
Morrison Chambers, 32 Nassau Street, Dublin D02 YH68

A CIP catalogue record for this book is available from the British Library

ISBN: 978-0-241-44877-9

www.greenpenguin.co.uk

MIX
Paper from
responsible sources
FSC® C018179

Penguin Random House is committed to a
sustainable future for our business, our readers
and our planet. This book is made from Forest
Stewardship Council® certified paper.

For Es

There was an inevitability about their road towards one another which encouraged meandering along the route.

Zadie Smith

Prologue

The barbershop was strangely quiet. Only the dull buzz of clippers shearing soft scalps. That was before the barber caught you watching her reflection in the mirror as he cut her hair, and saw something in her eyes too. He paused and turned towards you, his dreads like thick beautiful roots dancing with excitement as he spoke:

'You two are in something. I don't know what it is, but you guys are in something. Some people call it a relationship, some call it friendship, some call it love, but you two, you two are in something.'

You gazed at each other then with the same open-eyed wonder that keeps startling you at various intervals since you met. The two of you, like headphone wires tangling, caught up in this *something*. A happy accident. A messy miracle.

You lost her gaze for a moment and your breath quickened, as when a dropped call across a distance gains unexpected gravity. You would soon learn that love made you worry, but it also made you beautiful. Love made you Black, as in, you were most coloured when in her presence. It was not a cause for concern; one must rejoice! You could be yourselves.

Later, walking in the dark, you were overcome. You told her not to look at you because when your gazes meet you cannot help but be honest. Remember Baldwin's words? *I just want to be an honest man and a good writer.* Hmm. Honest man. You're being honest, here, now.

You came here to speak of what it means to love your best friend. Ask: if *flexing* is being able to say the most in the fewest number of words, is there a greater flex than love? Nowhere to hide, nowhere to go. A direct gaze.

The gaze requires no words at all; it is an honest meeting.

You came here to speak of shame and its relation to desire. There should be no shame in openly saying, *I want this*. There should be no shame in not knowing what one wants.

You came here to ask her if she remembers how urgent that kiss was. Twisted in her covers in the darkness. No words at all. An honest meeting. You saw nothing but her familiar shape. You listened to her gentle, measured breaths and understood what you wanted.

It is a strange thing, to desire your best friend; two pairs of hands wandering past boundaries, asking forgiveness rather than permission: 'Is this OK?' coming a fraction after the motion.

Sometimes, you cry in the dark.

I

The first night you met, a night you both negate as too brief an encounter, you pull your friend Samuel to the side. There's a bunch of you in the basement of this south-east London pub. A birthday celebration. Most on their way to drunk, or jolly, depending on which they'd prefer.

'What's up?'

'I don't normally do this.'

'Usually means this is something you've done before.'

'No, promise. Pinky promise,' you say. 'But I need you to introduce me to your friend.'

You'd like to say that in this moment, the older gentleman spinning records had faded something fast, something like Curtis Mayfield's 'Move On Up', into something equally so. You'd like to say it was the Isley Brothers, 'Fight the Power', playing when you expressed a desire you did not wholly understand, but knew you must act upon. You'd like to say, behind you, the dance floor heaved and the young moved like it was the eighties, where to move in this way was but one of a few freedoms afforded to those who came before. And since you're remembering this, the liberty is yours. But you did promise to be honest. The reality was you were so taken aback by the presence of this woman that you first reached to shake her hand, before opening up for the usual wide embrace, the result an awkward flapping of your arms.

'Hi,' you say.

'Hello.'

She smiles a little. You don't know what to say. You want to fill the gap but nothing comes. You stand, watching each other, in a

3

silence that does not feel uncomfortable. You imagine the look on her face is mirroring yours, one of curiosity.

'You're both artists,' Samuel says, a helpful interruption. 'She's a very talented dancer.' The woman shakes her head. 'And you?' she says. 'What do you do?'

'He's a photographer.'

'A photographer?' the woman repeats.

'I take pictures, sometimes.'

'Sounds like you're a photographer.'

'Sometimes, sometimes.'

'Coy.' Shy, you think. You leap across the conversation and watch as she darts after you. A red light leans across her face, and you catch a glimpse of something, something like kindness in her open features, her eyes watching your hands talk. It's a familiar tongue you note, definitely south of the river. Definitely somewhere you'd be more likely to call home. In this way there are things which you both know and speak with your very being, but here go unsaid.

'Do you want a drink? Can I get you a drink?' You turn, noticing Samuel for the first time since the conversation started. He's receded, slumped a little; he's smiling, but his body betrays he's feeling shut out. Feeling the sting of guilt, you try to welcome him back in.

'Do you guys want drinks?'

The woman's face splits open with genuine, kind amusement and, as it does so, there's a hand on your elbow. You're being pulled away; you're needed. The dance floor has cleared a little and there is a silence filled with all that is yet to come. There's cake and candles and an attempted harmony during 'Happy Birthday'. You slide your camera from where it swings on your shoulder, training your lens on the birthday girl, Nina, as she makes a wish, the solitary candle on her cake like a tiny sunshine. When the crowd begins to disperse, you are tugged in every direction. As the solo cameraman, it is your duty to document.

The music starts up once more. People stand in small bunches, pausing as you focus in on kind faces looming in the darkness. The older gentleman spinning records continues on at pace. Idris Muhammad's 'Could Heaven Ever Be Like This' fits.

Emerging from the crowd, you stand at the bar and crane your long neck in several directions. It is here, when you seek the woman once more, on the night in question, a night you both negate as too brief an encounter, you realize she is gone.

These are winter months. A warm winter – the night you met her, you misjudged the distance from the station to the pub and, having walked half an hour wearing only the shirt on your back, arrived self-conscious of the sweat on your forehead – but a winter nonetheless. It is the wrong season to have a crush. Meeting someone on a summer's evening is like giving a dead flame new life. You are more likely to wander outside with this person for a reprieve from whatever sweatbox you are being housed in. You might find yourself accepting the offer of a cigarette, your eyes narrowing as the nicotine tickles your brain and you exhale into the stiff heat of a London night. You might look towards the sky and realize the blue doesn't quite deepen during these months. In winter, you are content to scoop your ashes away and head home.

You mention the woman to your younger brother, who had been at the party too, building him an image from what you remember of the evening, like weaving together melodic samples to make a new song.

'But wait – I didn't see her?'

'She was tall. Kinda tall.'

'OK.'

'Wearing all black. Braids under a beret. Real cool.'

'Yeah, I'm getting nothing.'

'The bar looks like this.' You form an L-shape with your arms. 'I'm standing here,' you say, indicating the crook of the L.

'Hold on.'

'Yes?' you say, exasperated.

'Will it help or hinder if I tell you I was steaming that evening and remember nothing, full stop?'

'You're useless.'

'No, I'm just drunk. A lot. So what happens next?'

'What do you mean?'

You're both sitting in your living room, nursing cups of tea. The needle on the record player scratches softly at the plastic at the end of the vinyl, the rhythmic bump, bump, bump a meditative pulse.

'You meet the love of your life –'

'I didn't say that.'

' "I was at this party and I felt this, this presence, and when I looked over, there was this girl, no, this woman, who just took my breath away." '

'Go away,' you say, flopping back onto the sofa.

'What if you never see her again?'

'Then I'll take a vow of celibacy and live in the mountains for the rest of my life. And the next.'

'Dramatic.'

'What would you do?'

He shrugs, and stands to flip the record. A firmer scratch, like nail against skin.

'There's something else,' you say.

'What?'

You gaze at the ceiling. 'She's seeing Samuel. He intro'd us.'

'Huh?'

'I only found out after we'd spoken. I don't think they've been together long.'

'Is that a definite thing?'

'I mean, I think so, yeah. I saw them kissing in the corner of the bar.'

Freddie laughs and raises his hands.

'Yeah, I'm not judging you, man. Nothing is straightforward. But yeah, you might wanna –' He mimes scissors with his fingers.

How does one shake off desire? To give it a voice is to sow a seed, knowing that somehow, someway, it will grow. It is to admit and submit to something which is on the outer limits of your understanding.

But even if this seed grows, even if the body lives, breathes, flourishes, there is no guarantee of reciprocation. Or that you'll ever see them again. Hence, the campaign for summer crushes. Even if you leave each other on an unending night, even if you find your paths splitting ways, even if you find yourself falling asleep alone with but the memory of intimacy, it will be a shaft of summer creeping through the gap in your curtains. It will be a tomorrow in which the day will be long and the night equally so. It will be another sweatbox, or a barbecue with little food and more to drink. It will be another stranger grinning at you in the darkness, or looking at you across the garden. Touching your arm as you both laugh too hard at a drunken joke. Breathlessly falling through the door, gripping onto folds of flesh, or silently trying to locate the toilet in a home which isn't your own. In the winter, more times, you don't make it out of the house.

Besides, sometimes, to resolve desire, it's better to let the thing bloom. To feel this thing, to let it catch you unaware, to hold onto the ache. What is better than believing you are heading towards love?

3

You lost your grandma during the summer you were sure you could lose no more. You knew before you knew. It wasn't thunder's distant rumbling like a hungry stomach. It wasn't the sky so grey you were worried the light would not shine again. It wasn't the strain in your mother's voice, asking you not to leave home before she got there. You just knew.

You return to a memory of a different time. Sitting behind the compound in Ghana, where embers of heat so late in the day make you sweat. As your grandma sits on a rickety wooden stool, chopping ingredients for a meal to be prepared, you'll tell her that you met a stranger in a bar, and you knew before you knew. She will smile, and laugh to herself, keeping her amusement contained, encouraging you to go on. You'll tell her how this woman was slight, but tall, carried herself well, not in a way as to intentionally intimidate or placate, but in a way that implied sureness. She had kindness on her features and didn't mind when you hugged her.

What else? your grandma will ask.

Hmm. You'll tell her that when you and the stranger introduced yourselves, you both played down the things you did, the things you loved. Your grandma will pause at this detail. Why? she'll ask. You don't know. Perhaps it was because you had both lost that year, and though you kept telling yourself you couldn't lose any more, it continued to happen.

So? There's no solace in the shade, your grandma will say.

I know, I know. I think both of us kinda negate that whole encounter. It was too brief. There was too much going on. It wasn't the right time.

Your grandma will put down the knife, and say, It's never the right time.

You'll sigh and gaze towards a sky which shows no signs of darkening, and say, I guess there was something in the room that night, which I didn't feel until I met her. Something which, looking back, I couldn't ignore.

When you sow a seed, it will grow. Somehow, someway, it will grow.

Mmm. I agree. I just . . . I met this woman and she wasn't a stranger. I knew we had met before. I knew we would meet again.

How did you know?

I just knew.

And in this place, a memory from a different time, you would like to believe your grandma will be satisfied with this. That she will give the same wry, contained smile and laugh to herself again.

4

You and the woman meet in a bar, two days before 2017 comes to a close. You suggested the location, but you are late. Only by a minute or two, but late. You apologize; she doesn't seem to mind much. You embrace, and the conversation flows freely as you climb a set of stairs, travel up an escalator. You're a little breathless, a little sweaty, but if she notices, she doesn't say anything, not with her mouth nor roving eyes.

When you settle down, it's on a green felt sofa, made of two halves. You dance through topics like two old friends, finding comfort in a language which is instantly familiar. You create a small world for yourselves, and for you both only, sitting on this sofa, looking out at the world which has a tendency to engulf even the most alive.

'Last time we met, you said you were a photographer,' she says.

'No, someone told you I was a photographer, and I squirmed at the idea,' you say.

'Why?'

'You did the same when your dancing was brought up?'

'You didn't answer my question.'

'I dunno,' you say. 'But yeah, I take photographs.' On the other side of the window, Piccadilly bustles. A man swells his bagpipes, the sound drifting up towards you. Friday evening and the city is bordering on frenzy, unsure of what to do with itself.

'I guess,' you start up. 'I guess, it's like knowing that you are something and wanting to protect that? I know I'm a photographer, but if someone else says I'm that, it changes things because what they think about me isn't what I think about me. Sorry, I'm rambling.'

'I get what you're saying. But why does what someone else thinks about you change what you think about you?'

'It shouldn't.'

'You're very good at not answering questions.'

'Am I? I don't mean to be.'

'I'm playing with you,' she says, and indeed the smile in your direction is light and teasing.

'It's –' You pause, frowning to yourself as you reach for the right expression. 'You can't live in a vacuum. And when you let people in and you make yourself vulnerable, they're able to have an effect on you. If that makes sense.'

'It does.'

'What about you? The dancing thing?'

'Mmm. Maybe later. We keep digressing.'

'We do.'

'What do you think? About my idea? I want to document people, Black people. Archiving is important, I think. But as I said, I don't know the first thing about photography, and it would be cool to have you involved. Could be cool to do together.'

'Erm,' you say, letting the silence stretch and hold. 'I, yeah, no. No, I don't think I want to do it.'

'Huh?' Less of a question, more an involuntary noise. She sinks into the sofa, covering her whole self with her coat, and you watch it rise and fall like a duvet over a sleeping body.

'Hey,' you say. A forehead appears, followed by a strong set of eyebrows and a pair of eyes, wary and watchful. You watch her struggle with her discomfort.

'I'm joking. I'll do it. I wanna do it.'

The struggle continues and, when her face changes, it is because of reluctant appreciation. A jester meeting her match.

'I hate you. So much. So so much.' She checks the time. You've been sitting here for almost two hours.

'Should we have a drink? To celebrate this new . . . partnership? I need a drink.'

You're glad she asked.

You move from the mezzanine to the ground floor of the bar. The night is trailing after you, unable to keep up. A pair of low-bowled glasses sits half full on the table in front of you. They aren't your first, or second, or third drink. You are a little dizzy, trying to grasp what is happening. Much of your joy is lost in the need to hold it, intact, so you try to dull that voice which needs clarity, taking another sip. This is fine, you think, this feels right. She returns from the toilet, taking long strides towards you. The reflection of Leicester Square's lights dances on the glass. She reaches up, fingertips grazing the window, as if light is something that can be held. As she does so, her balance shifts, and her head makes a slow descent into your lap, coming to rest for a tender moment. And as she comes, she goes, giggling as she rises up to reach for the elegant glow.

This night is also the first you see the lazy sheer sheen which sits on her eyes when she's been drinking. Sweet conversation from sour lips, the salt on the rim of the glass perched on the tongue.

Later, you are in the Shake Shack next to Leicester Square. You stand in the queue, two sheets to the wind, swaying in a man-made breeze. You pay for the food – she bought the last round of drinks – and huddle together on a pair of high chairs. She orders a burger with chopped chillis, cheesy fries which she can't finish and insists you do (she hates wasting food). During the first few bites, she untangles a pair of white headphones and offers an ear, slender fingers dancing across her phone screen, searching for music. And now let's ask the general public: Was anyone in Shake Shack that night? Did anyone else see or hear two strangers performing their truths for each other? Did they fill the

13

pockets of the beat? Did they ride Kendrick's jazz-infused masterpiece with the same energy he intended?

On the way back to south-east London, a small joy, but a joy nonetheless. You ricochet through the dark underbelly of London. Noisy, black, hot and hellish. You peel back layers like a hand splitting the soft flesh of fruit. Beside you, she once more is working on a sailor's knot in her earphones. The hitch comes undone with a silent twang, and she slides one bud in her ear, the other in yours. Two people closing a distance made shorter by the trailing wires holding them together.

'What's your favourite song?' she asks, having to lean in to make herself heard over the Underground.

Above ground, you are comfortable with the theatrics of playing yourselves. When she tells you she attended the concert in question, you walk away for a moment, returning to her, feigning playful anger, feeling real envy. You speak, quick and urgent, as you weave down the uneven cobbles towards Embankment.

'My best friend had a pair of tickets, and agreed I could have the other –'

'But?'

'But the day before, he'd been like, *there's a girl . . .*'

'Ah. If it makes it any better, he is such a good performer.'

'Cheers.'

'You seem upset,' she says, unable to control the smile from tugging on her lips.

'I am.' And she listens, carefully, as you describe the significance of Isaiah Rashad's debut album, listing his influences and dissecting his musical style with breathless excitement.

'He's like an OutKast by way of J Dilla, with a sprinkle of Gil, the soul of an Isley Brother, so much soul in his music, you can really feel it, no? What?'

'Nothing.'

She's grinning as you follow her through the ticket barrier.

You don't tell her that the album had soundtracked your previous summer. You don't tell her that you had repeated the song 'Brenda', an ode to the artist's grandma, so much so that you knew when the bassline would begin to slide under the strum of guitar chords, when the trumpet would riff and reverb, when there was a break, a slight pause where the music fell loose from its tightly wound rhythm. You don't tell her that it was there, in the slight pauses, that you were able to breathe, not even realizing you were holding air in, but you were. There would be a moment where you exhaled and a small, sad smile spread on your face as you struggled to contain your own loss.

Below ground, you scroll through the tracklist, and point instead towards 'Rope/Rosegold'. She nods appreciatively.

'Mine's "Park". Such a big song.' She wheels up your favourite first, and locks her phone screen, turning up the volume as loud as it will go. You both know all the words. So much soul. A Black couple watch on, amused, as the pair of you play rapper for the short journey. Embankment to Victoria. A song's worth. You make it worth it, swaying with the twists and turns of the carriage, catching the swing of the rhythm, sitting in the pocket of the beat. A small joy, but a joy nonetheless.

You feel you have never been strangers. You do not want to leave each other, because to leave is to have the thing die in its current form and there is something, something in this that neither is willing to relinquish.

The view from her balcony: London's glittering skyline. You feel comfortable here. You feel at home.

'Tea?' she asks from the kitchen.

You nod, walking across the living room, to touch the glass. As if light is something you can hold, as if this is a painting you could touch. She appears noiselessly beside you.

'How long have you lived here? I'm jealous.'

'Couple years. It's all right, isn't it?' She hands you a mug and signals to her sofa. You both sit on opposite ends, knees pushed towards your chests, careful not to breach the border of the bisecting cushion; except you both know something has opened, like pressing at a teabag and gazing into the cup to find the leaves swarming through boiling water.

'Your mum is hilarious,' you say.

'She's not usually that friendly with strangers,' she says, sliding her legs out to sit in the space beside you. She closes her eyes and lets an almighty yawn stretch through the silence. It's contagious and she laughs as the baton is passed in a race only sleep will win. Her phone buzzes. A sound slips from her that you cannot quite work out.

'Are you OK?'

'I think Samuel is coming over.'

'Ah, right. Right.' Reality. 'I should go.'

'No, it's cool, you should finish your tea at least –'

'I don't want to impose –'

The doorbell rings.

After the door opens and shuts, after the fumbling of shoes being taken off, Samuel enters the living room. The night you all met in the basement of that south-east London pub returns to you: that need to know that woman, the way you insisted towards her. It was Samuel who engineered this meeting tonight; his girlfriend asked if he knew any photographers and you were who he thought of first. But you're gazing at Samuel now and the shame is intense. Feigned surprise on his face. 'Oh, hey.'

'Hey,' you say.

'I've heard you had quite a night.'

'We did, we did. It was real nice.'

'I'm sure it was,' Samuel says. He walks over to his girlfriend, giving her a quick peck. 'I'm gonna make some tea.'

You turn to her. 'I'm gonna head.'

'I'll see you out,' she says. From the kitchen, Samuel watches you watching her. You were careful not to breach a border, except you all know something has opened; the seed you pushed deep into the ground has blossomed in the wrong season. You think of how you will tell this story to those who ask, because there will be questions. You wonder if *it felt right* will be sufficient. You wonder if the defence of *nothing happened* will be sufficient.

It is the early hours of the morning. She dons an enormous green coat and walks you down the stairs. The night is as warm as her embrace and, as you pull away, she asks:

'Will you text me?'

'Of course.'

5

You say:

The sky has erupted and there's white ash on the ground. The dog has never seen snow before. It alternates between bounding across the icy planes and staying stock-still, aside from the tiny shake in its hind legs. Your grandma had never seen snow until the year you were born, while she awaited your arrival, and those tender flakes fell in a furious storm, clumping on the ground. She got on her knees and began to pray, for herself, her daughter and unborn grandchild. On the same day, your mother was on the top deck of a bus, cowering as a man waved a gun, and she emerged unscathed. You're not religious, but when you hear stories like that, it makes a man want to believe. You imagine your grandma in fervour, praying for your body barely formed, your spirit in gestation. Now her body is falling apart, or rather, has already fallen. Her spirit is everywhere. You don't know if you'll ever return and see where she has been laid to rest, but on this occasion, you do not have the strength. You're not religious but you're praying for your own mother and father as they make the journey back to Ghana, back home. Your knees are on hard wooden floor, prostrating at the foot of your own desires, when the dog nudges you in the back. The dog has never seen snow before. The sheet above is cloudless, lacking in form and detail. Have you ever looked at the sky at night after it has snowed? Orange glow, light caught between somewhere. Makes you want to reach up and touch, so sometimes, you pray. If prayer is mostly desire from the inner self, then you're praying for a safe trip for her.

*

She says:

There's nobody here to hear the soft pad of her feet across gold dust. Warm rush of the ocean. Just needed to get away. Just needed some peace of mind. Just needed to breathe. Sky here is cloudless too. The blue of a heatwave. Summer in January. Funny how time works.

Pulled herself over all sorts of lines to get here. Drew this line from herself to him, her father, all by herself, just to be close. No, the line was there, is always there, will always be there, but she's trying to reinforce, to strengthen. Blood and bone across the water, across continents and borders. What is a joint? What is a fracture? What is a break? It's all very difficult. Language fails us, especially when he doesn't open his mouth. It's all just, a lot. So she's reaching into a pocket of time, where there's nothing but heatwave blue, a summer in January, golden dust stuck between toes, the roar of a quiet body of water.

Also, a thank you. She's grateful.

You say:

There's a piece of art which comes to mind by Donald Rodney, titled *In the House of My Father*. A photo: a dark hand, palm turned upwards, lifelines criss-crossing skin; in the centre of the palm, a tiny house, loosely constructed, held together with several pins. You've often had such an image, or something similar, where you are made aware that you carry the house of your father, which means you also carry a part of the house he carried, your father's father's, and that this man would've done the same. Your first instinct is to ball your hand into a fist, crushing the thing, letting the weight drift to the ground; but perhaps it would be necessary to prise open its doors, to search the rooms which are lit, glance into those which are not, to see what, as of yet, remains unseen. Then leave this place, in peace, with peace, both his and yours, intact.

You know what it means to have to draw the line yourself.

You know what it means to have rugged anger melt, when your father laughs so hard at his own joke that tears stream down, down, down. You know what it means to find tears streaming down, down, down. Caught you unawares. A few years ago, and you had to turn off into an alley in the darkness and cry. The rush of memories like the tow of the ocean, the recollection of a man for whom love was not always synonymous with care. You cried like the time he left you in the shop and did not return. You cried yourself hoarse and soft. You cried like an infant does for their father. How ironic. Indeed, what is a joint? What is a fracture? What is a break? Under what conditions does unconditional love become no more? The answer is you will never not cry for your father.

You don't always like those you love unconditionally. Language fails us, always. Flimsy things, these words. And everything flounders in the face of real gratitude, which even a *thank you* cannot surmise, but a thank you to her also.

She says:

Language fails us, and sometimes our parents do too. We all fail each other, sometimes small, sometimes big, but look, when we love we trust, and when we fail, we fracture that joint. She doesn't want it to break and maybe that's not possible, but she doesn't want to find out. She's not religious either, but she knows what she desires.

She's looking forward to returning home, to a place familiar, where coherence and clarity might make an appearance.

6

'Have you eaten?'

'Nah, man.'

'I'll order. Chinese, Indian, Thai, Caribbean?' you ask.

'It'll never arrive if you order Caribbean. Chinese?'

'Chinese is always a safe bet,' you say.

You have the phone tucked between your ear and shoulder, supermarket shopping basket swinging from the other arm.

'What do you want? From the takeaway,' you add.

'Send me the menu. Actually, just something with chicken in it. Or no, ribs. Get me ribs, please.'

'Done deal. I'll see you soon.'

Back home, in your kitchen, you unpack the bag of things you know she likes but don't normally have stocked: those sweet chilli crisps, soy milk, Earl Grey teabags. You're only going to look over the sample images you took the week before, for the photography project you're working on together, but you would like her to feel comfortable, like her to feel at home.

Your house is too quiet, or rather it is loud in the absence of others. Your parents are still in Ghana, celebrating your grandma's life. Your little brother has returned to university. You're home alone. The silence is something you normally crave in such a full household, but something is missing. Every time you're at hers, you can guarantee the portable speaker is sending sound through the room. What to play? What says you're not overthinking this? Probably not having that thought, but it is too late now.

When the knock comes, it is a stout, smiling man, holding a brown paper bag soiled by oil. She rounds the corner your house sits on in a hurry, coming through the gate as the delivery man exits.

'Sorry, sorry.' You hug on your doorstep and, as you pull away, she says, 'Can I be honest?'

'Go on.'

'I don't really have an excuse. I'm just late. Was being lazy.'

'You're all good. Come in.'

She takes in her surroundings like a traveller mapping new lands. You watch her eyes graze over the photographs hanging in the hallway, working out what leads where, quickly gaining her bearings.

'Just you, your mum and dad?'

'My little brother too. He's at uni but comes home for the holidays. And whenever he wants, to be honest.'

'What's the age difference? This him?' She points to a photo of you and him, arms around each other's shoulders, mid-laughter, taken at a wedding the year before.

'Five years,' you say, nodding. On some days, like today, when he called and teased you about her coming over, the gentle ribbing descending into a back and forth which is never sharp, always underscored by rhythmic giggles which don't quite match your large bodies, on some days, like today, the distance is short and easy. This is your brother, partner in crime, stubborn opponent, gentle man. And on other days, like today, in the same phone conversation, when the laughter broke and you could hear him gulping for air, could hear the panic in his body trying to rise, could hear the tears, and he asked you to help him, to care for him, which wasn't a problem, is never a problem, except you have been doing it for years, especially when your father's love failed, when your father was far, in body or in spirit, and the responsibility fell to you, without much choice, and it was hard, difficult for a child to take care of himself and another, impossible to do without one or other being neglected, on other days, like today, you're reminded the

22

distance is long and hard. This is your brother, your charge, your duty, your son.

'You are a carbon copy of your mum,' she says. She gazes at a photo of your dad, but doesn't ask, so you do not tell.

She continues to map her route using familiarity, heading towards the kitchen to fill the kettle.

'Tea?'

'Shouldn't I be the one asking you?'

'Well, I'm here now.' She tries one cupboard, then another, and finds the Earl Grey. She catches you smiling.

'What?'

You shake your head. 'Where are you heading later?'

'Back to my old school. It's a bit of a journey.'

'You doing alumni stuff? Talking to the kids?'

She laughs. 'Something like that. Milk?'

'No, thank you,' you say, opening the fridge and passing her the carton of soya. 'I had to do something similar last year.'

'Where'd you go to school?'

'In Dulwich.'

She stops. 'You went to *that* school?'

'Not that one, but one close to it. Same foundation. Similar group of people. Same set of fees.'

'How'd that happen? I'm interested.'

As luck would have it, through taking a different route. You didn't like the larger, single-sex school, with its sprawling grounds and a feeling of discomfort you may come to know as implicit bias. But the journey home, on an alternative route, trying to avoid roadworks, will yield a glimpse of the smaller, mixed-sex school. *Smaller* is a relative term here: you can't see how far back the school stretches, but judging by the immaculate lawn preceding the casual hulk of the red-brick main building, it will be larger than your prepubescent self can ever understand.

It'll be the last set of exams you sit, and the last offer you receive. The kind man – you'll learn that kindness is rarely enough, but equipped with a certain knowledge and awareness, it can be – talks to you about Arsenal and United in your 'interview'. In the main hall, he'll direct you towards the biscuits: thick, crumbly shortbread laid out in rows, served by a Jamaican woman with a single gold tooth, who you'll later befriend. Your mother doesn't tell you exactly what was said; the interviewing teacher never tells you what he wrote in the letter of recommendation to ensure you wouldn't pay for this elite secondary-school education. Before you leave, he shakes your small and slender hand, his large and vein-ridden, bringing you close, as if to embrace.

'We need more kids like you, young man.'

At your blank expression:

'We need more young Black kids. We really do.'

'O-kaayyy,' she says. 'This makes sense.'

'What does?'

'Why we get along so well. Same thing. Seven . . . interesting years.'

She glances at the countertop behind her, body primed to leap up and seat herself atop the counter, but decides against it.

'What was being at school like for you?' you ask.

'It was . . . a lot. I never felt unwelcome but there was always something I didn't feel privy to.'

You, too, were likeable for a myriad of reasons, many of which you couldn't comprehend. There should be no reason for the group of sixteen-year-olds to see your confused and lanky frame, unsure how you have managed to wander so far from the building which houses your cohort, and approach with the intention of friendship.

'You look lost, bro.'

'I am.'

24

'Where are you going?'

'Lower school.'

They walk you back, grateful for this makeshift security detail.

'Who is your form tutor?'

'Miss Levy.'

'What? She used to be our form tutor. Tell her we said hello.'

One of them studies you closer. 'He looks like Gabs, doesn't he? What you think, Andre?'

Andre gives a non-committal grunt. Gabs, when you meet, is an enormous Nigerian boy, holding a quick-witted charm with an easy smile. The comparison is obvious, a little lazy. When faced with this supposed doppelgänger, there were questions: Do we look like each other? Are we all meant to be the same? Do you feel this strange feeling too, Gabs, the physicality of it, something hard and heavy at the top of your chest, like a shot of something clear which won't slip down? And if so, do you have a name for it?

Instead of an impromptu Q and A, you perform a complicated, natural handshake, to the glee of lookers-on. You don't say much to each other, but nod as you depart, understanding what has gone unsaid.

'Can I ask –'

'Three. Me and two other girls. You?' You're on the sofa now. She knocks your hand with her knee as she bunches her limbs up to assume a cross-legged pose. She's miscalculated, or perhaps this is a precise manifestation of desire unspoken; either way, neither of you say anything as her leg rests against yours, your hand now lazing atop her thigh.

'Four. Two boys, two girls. Year below me didn't have any,' you say.

'Lonely, no?'

Like Baldwin said, you begin to think you are alone in this, until you read. In this instance, two books are being spread open along the spine, despite the fact you don't remember some of these pages. She's looking at you and there is nowhere to hide here, nowhere to go. An honest meeting.

'Sometimes. Had some good people, though. And I found ways of coping,' you say.

'Yeah?'

'Yeah. You would find me either in the library or on the basketball court.'

'Of course, you played basketball.'

An activity which seems wholly arbitrary yet is anything but. The first time, you all stood in a semicircle and your coach showed you the moves – a bounce, pick up, two steps, extend towards the hoop, soft against the backboard, the ball slipping through the net. He told you it wouldn't come straight away, no, this would take practice. The confusion when you picked the ball up and did it the first time. Do it again. It wasn't a fluke. You just *got* it.

How does one articulate a feeling? There was a sensuality to the sharp movements you took towards the basket. Feeling rather than knowing; not knowing and feeling it was right. The moment slipped and shed. You had new skin. Bypassed something, the trauma, the shadow of yourself. This was pure expression. The steps were quick and sure like the intention of brush on canvas. No, you didn't *just* put a ball through a hoop. You received a new way of seeing, a new way of being.

It made you skinny, that game, that life. The T-shirt hugged your chest, long, strong arms hanging loose out of the material. Time will do that. You measured time in how quickly you could get up and down the court, the squeak of rigid rubber soles an aural stopwatch. In the last few years, on Fridays, you were relegated to the smaller sports hall, where badminton lines criss-crossed with your scoring markers. Basketball was an afterthought in this space, the court boundaries pressed up against the walls. You had to crack open the fire-exit door to soften the sting of chlorine wafting in from the adjacent swimming pool. Warm in there too. Just you. Sometimes, a teammate would join for the first hour; when fatigue began to set into your bodies, they would depart, while you continued to work out angles, to shoot until the swish of the ball through the hoop gave the sound of a violent snap. Practice? *We talking bout practice?* You had no real understanding of your ability – a blessing, a curse – but knew that this was something you must do. Especially after the injury, your shoulder out of your joint like an unfastened button. Trauma makes you considerate.

You wanted to put a ball through a hoop, and repeat. You didn't want to have to think about what it meant to wander the unending acres of the grounds, the series of coincidences and conditions which confirmed your place there, loud in the silence. You didn't want to have to think about what was seen when you offered a grin in the corridor; the discrepancy between what they thought they knew and what was true scared you. You didn't want to play a game in which you had no say in the rules, or the arena.

So, you retreated – or let's say you advanced – to the basketball court. The move was to grow closer to yourself so this was progress, no? You wanted to carve a home here, on the wooden floor with fading markings. You wanted to stretch into the outer limits of your body and beyond. You wanted to be breathing so hard you became breathless. You wanted to sweat. You wanted to ache. You wanted to launch a ball from half court, the orange orb spinning quicker and quicker as it approached the basket; the net making a splash when leather hits string. You wanted to smile, raising your hands in jubilance. You just wanted to feel something like joy, even if it was small.

You just wanted to be free.

*

'And you?'

'And me?'

'What was your thing?'

'My *thing*?'

'You're making me sound crazy. Come on. Black kid at private school? We all had a way of staying sane. Even if it was just yours.'

She nods, appreciatively. 'I hear that. Dancing. That was my thing. Still is.' You feel her body ease into the sofa as she speaks. 'When someone sees you – I'm just talking about day to day, you know – you're either *this* or *that*. But when I'm doing *my* thing?' A pause, as memory holds her, warm, thick, comforting. 'When I'm doing my thing, I get to choose.'

The silence is similar to whatever memory has gripped her, and you're both content to swim in it for a moment. A distant grumble approaches and groans, like an oncoming train speeding through the station, and she asks, 'Shall we eat?'

The sky is darkening and it's late afternoon. She places the last dish in the drying rack and turns off the tap. 'Think I gotta get going soon.'

'Is that all you're wearing?' you say, in a way you hope sounds caring, not judgemental. It's here that you notice how tidy and slender her frame is. She's wearing a white polo neck and a black wraparound, black tights, and arrived with only the clothes on her body.

'Yeah,' she says, looking down. 'I'm gonna be cold, aren't I?'

'Take my hoody.'

'The black one? That's your favourite.'

'Take it. You can give it back or I'll come get it off you or whatever.'

'If you're sure?'

'I'll go grab it from my room.'

'Can I come?'

'Yeah.'

'Can you give me a piggyback upstairs?'

'Erm, sure,' you say. You turn, bending your knees slightly. Her fingers find tender purchase in the grooves between your collarbone and shoulder blades, and she takes refuge on your back, laying her cheek across the side of your neck. Her thighs in your hands, you make the short journey with ease.

'I'm not too heavy, am I?'

You shake your head as she dismounts. She wasn't heavy but there was a weight to her which didn't match the lean figure you studied in your kitchen. Which is to say there was more life in your hands than you expected.

'Jheeze.' She cranes her head ninety degrees to read the spines of the towers of books on your table. Takes a perch on the edge of your bed. Her eyes dance across the titles. 'I miss being able to read anything. I'm doing English Lit at uni,' she adds.

'Ah. Well, feel free to borrow anything.'

'I'm reading this great book at the moment: *The Same Earth* by Kei Miller. But I'll be back,' she says, here and not quite. 'Maybe,' reaching towards the smallest stack, a pile you always return to, 'for some Zadie.'

'Good choice.'

Bellingham station is a short walk away, and you cut through the park en route. In an enclosed area, four young men converge to play basketball on a day free of the mist and gloom spring can bring. Three are dressed for the occasion, one is not. The latter holds a tiny, yapping dog on a leash, while dispensing tips for success.

'Hold it with one hand . . . nah, that one is just for support. There you go.'

One of the other players, imbued with fresh knowledge, launches a shot skywards. The arc is nice, but as the ball spins through the air, it's clear theory will not marry practice. The ball misses everything it can: backboard, rim, net. The young man shrugs off the teasing, gathering the ball, assuming the position, willing to try again.

She falls into your stride as you make your usual journey – down the hill, through the park, along the main road of this tiny London town, complete with its Morley's and the off-licence, the Caribbean takeaway, the always empty pub – to the top of the small slope where the station waits.

'I guess this is goodbye.'

'For now,' you say, hoping the disappointment doesn't show. You don't want your time together to end.

'For now. I'll see you soon. I kinda have to now,' she says, tugging at the hoody. 'I'll link you before I go back to Dublin.'

The groan escapes before you can contain it.

'What?' she asks.

'That's far.'

'It is,' she says. 'I'll be back, though.' The train pulls in and she taps her Oyster card on the reader, stepping on board. You both wave as the doors close. She smiles at you as she settles into her seat, waving again. You begin to do the same, chasing after the train in pantomime fashion, spurred on by her laughter. You run and wave and laugh until the train gathers speed and the platform runs out. She escapes the frame, until it is just you on the platform, a little breathless, a little ecstatic, a little sad.

7

And it wasn't that day, or the day after, but sometime after that, you cried in your kitchen. You were alone in the house and had been for a week or so. Headphones sending sound into the silence, a tender croon stretched across drums designed to march you towards yourself. In an easy rhythm, the rapper confesses his pain, and so you stop and ask yourself, *How are you feeling? Be honest, man.* You're sweeping debris across the kitchen tiles, reaching into the corners for far-flung flecks. Moving the brush in an easy rhythm, you begin to confess, your joy, your pain, your truth. You dial for your mother but she is still far away, wrestling with the grief of her mother's passing. You want to tell her that you miss her mother, to confess that you lost your God in the days your grandma lost her body and gained her spirit, to tell her you couldn't face your own pain until now. She would need you intact, you think. You end the call you initiated. You dial for your father, but you know he will not have the words. He will hide behind a guise, he will tell you to be a man. He will not tell you how much he hurts too, even though you can hear the shiver in the timbre of his voice. You decline the call. You dial for your brother, but he too carries the house of your father. He will not have the words.

So you're in the kitchen, and you're alone, but this isolation is new. Something has come undone. You are scared. You know what you want but you don't know what to do. This pain isn't new but it is unfamiliar, like finding a tear in a piece of fabric. You cry so hard you feel loose and limber and soft as a newborn. You want to pull and push and mould yourself back together. The headphones slip from your head as you slide to the floor, loose and limber and soft. You're wailing like a newborn. You're alone. You don't feel in rhythm. There's nothing playing. The music has stopped. A break: also known as a percussion break. A slight pause where the music falls loose from its tightly wound rhythm. You have been going and going and going and now you have decided to slow down, to a halt, and confess. You are scared. You have been fearful of this spillage. You have been worried of being torn. You have been worried that you would not repair, would not emerge intact. You lost your God so you cannot even pray, and anyway, prayer is just confessing one's desire and it's not that you don't know what you want, it's that you don't know what to do about it. You're on your knees, and the music has stopped and you're wailing like a newborn. Your mother calls. You decline the call. She would need you intact and you are not so. You need to face this alone, you think. Something has come undone. Your cup has runneth over, and now it's empty, the flow has ceased, but you're still loose and limber and soft. You want to push and pull and mould yourself back together, so you rise from the cool kitchen tile. You stumble from kitchen to hallway, making it to your stairs. The wail has dwindled but you still feel tender. You gaze at the mirror on the wall, and though the music has stopped and the rhythm has fallen away, you confess your joy, your pain, your truth. You stop and ask yourself, how are you feeling?

The song which had been playing when the wobble became a spill was 'Afraid of Us' by Jonwayne, featuring a vocal sample from a group of Black women, one of whom was Whitney Houston's mother, Cissy. In isolation, the hum of the melody raises the hairs on the arm, raises something within you. Have you ever been afraid of what lies within you, what you're capable of? Anyway, when you mop up the spill and all that remains is a shiny kitchen tile and your delicate body, made soft by your tears, you stand in your living room, listening to 'Junie' by Sol-ange. You raise your arms in casual jubilance, thankful to be alive. Such simplicity in gratitude. Simple progression too in this ode to funk singer Junie Morrison. Which is to say everything comes of something else. Which is to say from your solid ache comes a gentle joy. Which is to say, moving across your living room, affording yourself the freedom, to be, such simplicity in this, in the hazy, rhythmic bounce of the drums, intentional bassline, intentional and unthinking in your steps, approaching ecstasy, losing control of what you know, losing what you know. Born fresh, born new, born free. Bypassing something, the trauma, the shadow of yourself. This is pure expression. Ask yourself here, as you begin to move with quick, light steps, bare feet sliding across the floor, a delicate sweat forming: ask yourself here, how are you feeling?

The previous summer you asked the same question and found thin mist obscuring your form and detail. You found yourself in your room, unaware of the ache until you stood and felt a twinge in your side like a stray thorn had pierced you. You quietly got dressed and took a bus from Bellingham to Deptford, to a bar underneath the dim arches of the station, where musicians were said to gather and, channelling their voices through their various instruments, ask each other, how are you feeling?

You were annoyed at your own haze, at your lack of form and detail. But you made a choice, to be there, to want to shift, to want to move, and there was power in reaching towards yourself in this way. You thought about the intention of being, and how that could be a protest. How you were all here, protesting; gathered together, living easy. Spilling drinks on pavements. Two for £10. You're all drinking now, but you weren't allowed earlier, no, that table was reserved, all night, you just wanted a drink before the party next door, but no, your business was no good for them. You swallowed this and gathered together, easy living. Spill a drink on the pavement, the foam washing over blacktop like ocean spray.

The music drew you all inside. There's a way to play the drums that makes hips move and feet jump. When one friend – first-timer – asked another – veteran – what it was like, she said, 'The ancestors visit us and we let them take over.' Maybe the ancestors are always within and you let them emerge. You saw it in the head rising above a curly mane of hair. You saw it in the hopping shoulders, the delicate curve of the spine. You saw it in the sweat pooling in the tiny waves of baby curls, at the bottom of a bunch of braids, nestled in the oiled frizz of natural hair; the rise and the fall of the Black body, no, the Black personhood, moving of its own accord, the beauty in her stamp, the nonchalant cheek on his playful features, the glint of a trumpet cradled by a dark hand in the light, an MC's lips grazing the microphone; you were losing something, it's not yourselves, no, but you were losing something, or perhaps it was like plunging into an ocean, the sticky tar of trauma washed away by the waves.

Dance, you said. Dance, sing, please, do what you must; look at your neighbour and understand they are in the same position. Turn to your neighbour and take one step forward as they take another step back, switch positions, move, move, move, become overwhelmed by the water, let it wash over you, let the trauma rise up like vomit, spill it, go on, let it spill on the ground, let go of that pain, let go of that fear, let go. You are safe here, you said. You are seen here. You can live here. We are all hurting, you said. We are all trying to live, to breathe, and find ourselves stopped by that which is out of our control. We find ourselves unseen. We find ourselves unheard. We find ourselves mislabelled. We who are loud and angry, we who are bold and brash. We who are Black. We find ourselves not saying it how it is. We find ourselves scared. We find ourselves suppressed, you said. But do not worry about what has come before, or what will come; move. Do not resist the call of a drum. Do not resist the thud of a kick, the tap of a snare, the rattle of a hi-hat. Do not hold your body stiff but flow like easy water. Be here, please, you said, as the young man took a cowbell, moving it in a way which makes you ask, which came first, he or the music? The ratata is perfect, offbeat, sneaking through brass and percussion. Can you hear the horns? Your time has come. Revel in glory for it is yours to do so. You worked twice as hard today, but that isn't important, not here, not now. All that matters is that you are here, that you are present, can't you hear? What does it sound like? Freedom?

8

'I've been feeling low.'

'Are you OK?'

You're lying on your bed, feet propped up against the wall, watching the ceiling like an unmoving sky. You're on the phone, reaching across the distance, not for the first time, nor the last. Her voice spins towards you through the soft static and you try to map its direction, imagining the soundwave drifting from a place you have never seen.

'Can I be honest?'

'Always.'

'I'm very tired.'

With your confession, the truth imbues your self with form and detail. You hear her low exhale and know she understands you're not tired in the way sleep will solve, no. You're weary. You're not without joy, but the pain is much, often. And like Jimmy said, you begin to think you are alone in this, until she says:

'Me too.'

'How do you cope?' you ask.

'I smoke. I drink. I eat. I try to treat myself often. I try to treat myself well. And I dance.'

'Tell me more about that. Please.'

'The smoking or the drinking?'

You both laugh and you hear her rearrange herself, perhaps sitting up.

'I like to move,' she starts. 'I always have. Used to catch me on the playground out-dancing *everyone*. It's my space, you know? I'm making space and I'm dancing into the space. I'm like, dancing into the space the drums leave, you know, between the kick and the snare and the hat, where that silence lies, that huge silence, those moments and spaces the drums are asking you to fill. I dance to breathe but often I dance until I'm breathless and sweaty and I can feel all of me, all those parts of me I can't always feel, I don't feel like I'm allowed to. It's my space. I make a little world for myself, and I live.'

'Wow.'

'Sorry, that was a lot.'

'No, don't apologize. I've never heard anyone talk about dance like that, it's cool. There's a night on Wednesdays in Deptford, really close to you . . . it's jazz music but there's something different in that room. An energy that's very . . . very freeing. A bunch of Black people just being themselves.'

'We should go when I'm back in London. There's nothing like that in Dublin.'

'Let's do it.'

You turn the phone on speaker and let your legs flop onto the bed. Resting your body on its side, both hands tucked underneath your head as if in prayer. Desiring peace. Your breathing eases. You hear hers too, both of you pushing and pulling, ebb and flow, the ocean separating you. Somewhere in the quiet rush, you hear a snore. You sign off quietly, hoping not to wake her.

9

'Do you want a biscuit?'

'Erm –'

'Go on. Take a couple.'

Her mother places a large silver tin on the tiny table in front of you, an assortment of biscuits stacked over each other. You take a pair of chocolate digestives, and dip one into your cup of tea. The biscuit softens and one half plops into your Earl Grey.

'What's on at the moment?' her mother asks no one in particular, pointing the remote at the television. Flicking through the channels, she settles on the Winter Olympics. You both watch four humans skitter around a racetrack, carved from solid blocks of ice, in a svelte vehicle shaped like a long smooth pebble.

You are here, at her house, for your hoody. You were meant to meet just before she returned to Dublin, but in this city, much will conspire to prevent meetings and appointments. It was a Sunday in February, and you both watched train after train cancel, before giving up. So now you're here, without her presence, which is heavier in her absence. You're here, in her house, for your hoody, which you expected to pick up and depart, back to your home, where it is just you, where the quiet is beginning to hum and buzz in a way you can hear.

When you came in, her mother welcomed you, and asked if you wanted a cup of tea. You watched her elegant yet determined shuffle, head down in concentration rather than dismay, opening cupboards, retrieving the biscuit tin.

'Ridiculous sport,' her mother says. The screen has changed.

A woman slowly launches a stone-shaped object across the ice, letting go of the curved grip mounted to the top. Two more women, armed with long-handled brushes, scrub at the ice as if they are trying to rid a stain. An invisible path is cleared and the object glides silently across the ice, entering a target zone with a white bullseye.

'Of course, hold on.' You hear her shuffling elsewhere in the house; when she comes back to the living room, she lays your hoody across one of the chairs.

'What have you been doing today?'

It's Saturday night. Elsewhere in the city, people are rebelling against their weekly duties, filling up pubs and bars and dance floors. Whatever warmth was teased earlier in the winter must have been delusion. You spent the day indoors, the morning slipping by at your desk where you flicked through a book of images – Roy DeCarava's *The Sound I Saw* – and you wrote a little, not much, but something, you wrote something. The rest of the day, a blanket draped over you, poring over the pages of a novel – Zadie Smith's *NW*.

'I love her writing,' her mother says.

'She's my favourite writer. *NW* is the book I return to most.' Perhaps that is how we should frame this question forever; rather than asking what is your favourite work, let's ask, what continues to pull you back?

Last year, on a summer's evening, you presented your battered copy of *NW* for Zadie to sign. A brown headwrap, gold hoops swinging from her ears, and something like knowing on her face, despite admitting earlier in the evening she was perpetually unsure. Her presence was peaceful, slow, sage-like. She could see you were a little awkward, a little overwhelmed – your friend will swear you were close to tears – and steered the conversation.

'Where's your family from?'

'Ghana.'

'Ah. My mother married a Ghanaian, briefly. You're wonderful people.'

'What happened? Your mother, I mean.'

'Some things aren't meant to work out.'

You spoke some more, and you tried – and failed – to explain what the book meant to you. That there were many similarities between your south-east London and her north-west.

'South-east – where?'

'Catford.'

'My grandma lived in Catford. I spent a lot of time there growing up.'

You smiled, while she signed your book, unable to say any more. Unable to tell her you have read her book many times and will do so many more. To tell her where your breath catches, where your eyes widen. That illustrations of desire slipped into the comfort of a paragraph did not go unnoticed. You want to say when you read her essay about this novel –

The happy ending is never universal. Someone is always left behind. And in the London I get up in – as it is today – that someone is more often than not a young Black man.

– that you understood.

Her mother's interest is piqued when you mention writing.

'What are you writing, fiction?'

'I dunno. Kind of. It's just to supplement my photography, really. Trying to find another form to tell stories with. But yeah, I spend a lot of time with novels.'

'So,' she says, crossing one leg over the other. 'There are really only two plot devices when writing: a stranger comes to town, or a person goes on a journey. All good work is just variations of these ideas.'

You ponder this when you leave. But what of *NW*, the book in which no one wins?

And what of the life you lead? Who is the stranger? Who is the familiar? And what are their journeys?

You didn't know whether to hug her mother when you were leaving but rode an instinct, wrapping long arms around her quickly, not lingering. She smelt of petrichor and a place you might grow to call home.

Waiting for the bus in the darkness, you pull on the hoody. It smells like her: sweet like the torn petal of a flower, sweet like lavender plucked from its stem while in summer bloom. You put your headphones on and load up Kelsey Lu's EP, *Church*, an album full of orchestral loops designed to reach towards a quiet ecstasy. You could be anywhere right now, your eyes closed, enveloped in her presence, which is heavier in her absence. But you are home, amongst the melody, slipping into percussive breaks, breathing easy.

10

You're riding the Overground, from Shoreditch to south-east London, when she calls. It snowed earlier in the day, a layer of white dust bordering on disruptive. Yet, when walking to the station, the only trace was in your memory, the ground wet now, the air crisp.

'Where are you?' she asks.

'I am . . .' You look outside and latch onto the enormous Sainsbury's. 'Pulling into Brockley.'

'I'm back from Dublin. Thank God for reading week.'

'I thought you were back on Monday?'

It's another Saturday night and the train is loud with a group of football fans talking at a level you're sure they have normalized across the course of the day.

'Nope, today. Who is that?'

You get up and walk towards the exit, cupping the microphone to your mouth.

'Bunch of guys. Palace fans, it looks like.'

'Why are you whispering?'

''Cause it's all good-natured but I don't want them to think I'm chatting about them.'

'Fair. Listen –'

'Yeah?'

'I think you should get in an Uber and come to mine.'

'You think,' you say, 'I should get in an Uber and come to yours?'

'Yes.'

'OK. I will.'

'OK. OK. When will I see you?'

The train pulls in a few moments later. As you run off the platform and into the street, weaving towards your taxi, you experience a strange moment in which you are flung into the future, wondering how you will remember this. You would like a witness. You would like someone to stop you and ask, *What are you doing?*, to which you would reply, *I'm doing what I feel.*

'Hey, friend.'

'Hey, friend.'

'I missed you,' you say.

'Did you now?'

'I did.'

'That's nice.'

'This is the part where you say, "I missed you too."'

'Eh – kinda.'

'Whatever.'

She beams and throws her arms around your neck, her mane of curly hair tickling your face as she pulls you close. Today, shea butter and coconut oil. As you separate, you point at her T-shirt.

'You drink Supermalt?'

'Absolutely not. That drink is horrid. My cousin gave me this shirt.'

'How can you not like Supermalt?'

'It's like a whole meal in a bottle. So heavy. It doesn't taste good either, tastes like . . .' She shudders, as if whatever she is trying to recall is traumatic.

'The Ghanaian in me is offended.'

'Unless you want to keep being offended, keep that drink away from me.' You walk through to her living room, she to the kitchen. 'Speaking of, have you eaten?'

'Unless you count the two ciders I had earlier, that's a no.'

'Let's get takeout. Pizza. Hot wings. Both.'

'Both?'

'Yeah.'

'Hmm,' you say, struggling to keep the smile from your voice.

'What?'

'You never finish food.'

She folds her arms and her features crumple in disdain.

'*You* never finish *your* food.'

'I always finish my food.'

'No, fair.' She shrugs. 'My eyes are bigger than my stomach. Anyway, that means I always have lunch the next day.'

'I'll give you that one,' you say, pulling up the takeout website. 'I feel like a big part of our foundation is eating and drinking together.'

'I don't think those are bad things to take pleasure in.'

'Neither, neither.'

When the food arrives, the doorbell buzzes, despite you leaving instructions to ring when they get here; she doesn't want to wake her mother. You hear her telling off the delivery man, fighting a battle she has already lost at the door.

She joins you on the sofa, setting the pizza box between you, tearing a slice away, holding out her hand to protect from the strings of cheese. You do the same, folding your slice in half so it becomes food and plate; she mimics you and lets out a sigh of hunger being sated. As she does so, reclining into the sofa, she reaches for your hand, and you take it, fitting together like this is an everyday. She's wearing rings on her fore and ring fingers, the bands cool between your own. Neither of you dare look at one another as you hold this heavy moment in your hands. You're light-headed, and warm. You're both silent. You're both wondering what it could mean that desire could manifest in this way, so loud for such a tender touch. It's she who breaks the moment.

'We can't eat holding hands like this.'

'My bad.'

'No one's bad.'

She switches on the TV, flooding the room with noise. It's a Spike Lee joint, so it's audacious and provocative and brash. A remake of his nineties film *She's Gotta Have It*. The couple on screen are having sex, loudly, but in a way that's too clean to reflect the intense mess of being intimate with another.

'You still having that dry patch?'

'Yessir,' she says. 'You?'

'Dry as an uncreamed elbow.' She bites her bottom lip but her eyes are grinning. 'Go on,' you say. 'You can laugh. But wait – you and Samuel only broke up a month ago.'

'Long enough,' she replies.

'Agreed.'

'I might give up soon.'

'I feel like celibacy is looking more appealing than trying at this point.'

'How long has it been?'

'Eight months.'

'Huh?'

'You heard me.'

'That's not a dry patch, that's a drought.'

You wonder what Samuel would think of this conversation. But then he doesn't mention anything to you, not any more. Since this friendship has blossomed, Samuel has withdrawn, growing more distant as the pair of you here grew closer. When they split, you checked in on him, but the calls did not go through, the messages went undelivered. Samuel had severed the connection. You wonder how he is feeling and what he would say if this was a picture he were privy to. You push the thoughts and any guilt away, laughing off the suggestion, reaching for another slice of pizza.

It's easier to do this, to open a box and close it quick, seal it with sharp quips. It's easier to let your bodies do the same, taunting and teasing, short grazes, soft sighs. Working yourselves into a feverish frenzy, your laughter knocking across the room,

45

the noise protecting your truths, or so you both think. You do this until you're both tired, and she stretches her long body across the sofa, her head resting in your lap. Heavy like the moment in your hands. You rest one hand on her scalp, reaching through the dense curls, the other settled between her waist and hip.

'Don't let me fall asleep,' she mumbles. Shortly after, you close your eyes too.

You wake in the early hours of the morning and it's like you're in the memory of the present. Something quiet from the speaker. Her head hot and heavy in your hands. Mouth dry, hazy vision. Your stirring lifts her from her sleep, and you can tell it's the same for her, trying to find lucidity in the mist.

'I need to get into bed,' she manages. 'You should stay.'

'OK,' you say. She rises and you stretch your limbs to replace the presence of hers. She shakes her head, and beckons.

You don't talk here, in her bedroom, where it's dark and hot and heavy, yet welcoming, like being clasped in an embrace by something much larger than you. She pulls down the blinds and draws the curtain, and now it's blackness, faint light of dusk spilling from the hallway. She waits for you to undo your belt, take down the buttons of your shirt, makeshift pyjamas of a vest and underwear, before she closes the door and thrusts you further into the dark. She climbs into bed by memory and you feel your way towards her. There's a little room to manoeuvre but she pulls you close. Your face rests on the pillow and she tucks her face into the curve of your neck. Your legs are tangled in order, hers, yours, hers, yours, and your arms curl around each other's backs. You fit, as if this has been your everyday. You don't talk here, in her bedroom, where it's dark and hot and heavy, making quick light steps towards sleep. You don't talk here, but even if you did, the words would fail you, language insufficient to reflect the intense mess of being this intimate with another.

You have to leave when light starts to sneak under the blinds. You wake and the fever has broken and left havoc in its place. Thoughts skip around your mind. Dry mouth, hazy vision. Your stirring doesn't wake her this time, but as you reach for her door handle, she lets out a small sound of protest. Takes your hand, reaching as she did, locking in, kissing the skin. There's nothing more to say here. You lean down and kiss the top of her head.

The next day, you're in the lift once more, rising to the sixth floor. You knock on her door. An open smile. You're shooting today for the project which started this all, and you feel a nervous shake as you embrace, but you don't know if it is because of the project or what happened last night. You're wondering how you would explain the latter to the witness you requested. *But nothing happened*, you would say. The witness would shake their head, as if to say, *Don't you know what that means?* Lying together, sober, with only the vague shape of her as a guide for existing, feeling safe. Is that what love is? The feeling of safety? And here you are, safe in her presence, separated only by each other's silence.

'How are you feeling?' you ask.

'I'm nervous. About this,' she says, pointing to the camera equipment you're setting up.

'You'll be fine. You've got this.'

'About us too.' A pause. 'Do we need to –'

The doorbell goes.

'Talk,' she says. 'I was gonna ask if we need to talk. But like, nothing happened, right?'

'Right. Nothing happened.'

'We're all good?'

'Definitely. Right?'

47

'Right.' The doorbell goes again.

'You should get that.'

'*You* should get that.' You both smile at the absurdity of it all. At the feeling of feeling absurd.

You spend the afternoon taking photos of her friend, who is a poet. Later, much later, you'll look up some of the poet's work, and find 'Before Leaving', a cyclical poem about things which go unsaid. A poem about comings and goings, and the gaps between a dial tone, those pauses like percussive breaks where your own breath is the loudest. The poet sees words unspoken in the embrace between you and her. The poet sees both the tremble in the water and the sinking stone which caused the ripple. The poet sees you, the poet sees her, and you're grateful for some lucidity in this mist.

You share a table at dinner, the three of you, and when you're departing, the poet who sees you and her, sees the ripple and the sinking stone, tells both of you to stay out of trouble.

The trouble is, that afternoon, a day after she arrived, a day after the fever dream began, you're taking photos and she looks towards you while the poet is talking. She loses concentration for a moment, and holds your gaze, for one, two, three, before recovering. When you get the images, you're sure you stopped breathing, and held the gaze, one, two, three, before recovering, a slight judder to the camera as you were jolted back to the present. The trouble is, this is trouble that you welcome. You realize there is a reason clichés exist, and you would happily have your breath taken away, three seconds at a time, maybe more, by this woman.

The trouble is, you are not only sharing dinner tables with her, you are in the process of beginning to share your life in a way you have not before. You're walking from the station to her house, the street lights dousing you in tough glares at intervals. You're talking about a play you have both seen, *The Brothers Size*. You saw it twice in its short London run, and both times found your breath robbed, hot tears trailing one after the other down your cheeks. It is a play about the conditions under which unconditional love *might* break; in the end, one finds they will never not cry for their brothers.

'I saw it too, and it got me, but I don't know if it got me like that,' she says.

'I helped raise my brother. I know what it's like to love like that. To have joy and to be pained, and sometimes to have real anger towards him. He's my best friend but sometimes he's like my son too.'

She doesn't look at you while you cry in the darkness but she does take hold of your hand, rubbing her thumb across the back. This closeness, this comfort, is enough.

II

The trouble is, the day after, the haze arrives like a night mist. You're sitting in the National Theatre with Isaac, amongst cold bricks and concrete, warm, fever unbroken. You're having difficulty concentrating. You long for her touch. The night before, you held each other in the same way.

'Do you have to leave?'

'I should. I have to return all this equipment kinda early.'

'How early?'

'He wants it by seven.'

'Shit, that is early.' She nestled closer, if that were possible. 'Will I see you tomorrow?'

'Definitely,' you said.

The trouble is, and let's explain this trouble, yes: you are tumbling in the heat of a fever dream, and you surface only to plunge once more. Donatien Grau's words: *When the mind is lost in ecstasy, there is no condition for self-reflection, self-questioning.* You're not asking yourself questions. You're not asking yourself about the conditions under which you and she met. You're not thinking of the night in the pub when you urged Samuel to introduce the pair of you. You're not thinking of the night you all found yourselves in her flat, your own attraction bright like a small flame. You're not thinking of the fact that that friend no longer considers you so, will not return your calls or text messages. You're not thinking of what it looks like. You're not thinking. You're feeling. You are in a memory of something yet to happen. You want to sigh with hunger sated. You want to hold her in the hot darkness. You want –

'You hear me? Wanna go to a show tonight?' Isaac asks.

'I'm meant to be seeing my friend,' you say.

'Your friend, huh?'

'My friend,' you insist, though who are you trying to convince? Isaac or yourself?

'Let's get drinks before, then. What time you seeing her?'

'How'd you know it's a woman?'

'This isn't my first rodeo.'

'What you mean?'

'You look like you got hit by a bus, and you dusted yourself off, and did it again for the hell of it. You look like you're wondering when the next time you can get hit by that bus is.'

'What a strange analogy.'

'Am I lying?'

No, he is not. You are back again, in a memory of something yet to happen. You want to sigh with hunger sated. You want to hold her in the hot darkness. You want your bodies to say what cannot be otherwise said.

Later that evening, she asks you to join her drinking in Bethnal Green. You don't think, announcing to your friends that you are leaving. Isaac looks on with a knowing glint in his eye, and says nothing.

'But you just bought a ticket to the show,' another friend says.

'Can I have it?' his companion says, having joined your group in the past few minutes.

'Done. Problem solved.'

You leave your friends, setting off at pace, through Soho towards Piccadilly Circus. Brown line to Oxford Circus, red line to Bethnal Green. You're drawing a line towards her. No, the line was there, is always there, will always be there, but you're trying to reinforce, to strengthen.

Your phone lets out a loud ping as you emerge from the Underground station.

Where are you?
Be there soon.

'I'm drunk,' she says when you slide alongside her at the restaurant. The sheen on her eyes is a giveaway, silver like mirrored glass. She takes your hand in hers, and rests it in your lap. In this way, she is drawing a line towards you; she has done so since this fever dream started. Or no, you drew the line towards her when you asked for an introduction. She drew the line back when she asked you to get an Uber to her house. The line was there, is always there, will always be there, but you're both trying to strengthen it.

It's happy hour at the bar, and she introduces you to her friends, Nicole and Jacob. An assortment of cocktail glasses clink and clunk and bump against one another, the tinkle of laughter a chaser. You're settling in, curling into each other, her head lolled on your shoulder, when Jacob points at you, then at her.

'So you two are a thing, right?'

'Pardon?'

'You two are . . .' He winks, obtusely.

If only he knew. This crude white man who has spent most of the time you have been at the table explaining his self-importance – he's in advertising, he tells you – is he to be your witness? Were you to lean over and explain that you and she were not a thing in the way that he thought, but in a way in which neither of you could comprehend? To tell him that the seed you pushed deep into the ground has blossomed in the wrong season, the flourish of the flower a surprise for you and her both?

'Come on,' he says. 'It's obvious.'

'What's obvious?' she says.

'You two are fucking.'

'Absolutely not.'

'You are.'

'We are *not*.'

'We're all friends here,' he gestures to the table. 'Two good-looking people, I don't see what's to hide.'

Perhaps this is not the witness but the man sent for you to confront yourselves.

'We're not having sex,' you say.

'Hmm,' the man says, taking a sip from his beer. 'Well, you'd make a good couple.' He smiles to himself. Her grip tightens around your hand. You hadn't noticed that you had been facing this man together until that moment.

'Wait, how did you two meet?' Jacob asks.

'A friend introduced us.'

'Your boyfriend?' Nicole asks, unhelpfully.

'Your boyfriend introduced you two?' Jacob is in danger of making his way to your side of the table.

'We're not together any more.'

'Oh dear,' he says, taking real pleasure.

In the fresh night air, walking hand in hand, she pulls you short. She takes a moment to steady herself, her eyes silver like mirrored glass, the reflection of yourself warped and warbled. You're standing here, on Brick Lane, on a Monday evening. She arrived on Saturday night, and you didn't think when you drew a line towards her. Did not think about continuing to return each day. Did not think as you reach a hand to her face and she nudges against your palm, a brief pleasure crossing her features. She stops and takes both your hands in hers.

'You have to promise nothing will change,' she says.

'I can't promise that.'

'You have to. I love you too much for this to change. You're like my best friend,' she slurs. 'You're so much more.'

'OK, OK,' you say, trying to steady yourself. 'I promise.'

Dim darkness of her room, blind pulled, curtains drawn. A bottle of water atop her chest of drawers to ward off a hangover.

Rarely enough, but no harm in trying. Anyway, she announces that she has to change into her pyjamas, and you turn away from her, because right now, the thing you crave to be lost in is not her flesh. She taps your shoulder and slips a hand onto your waist to turn you back to face her. She stands on your feet and lays her head against your chest, listening to your heart thud like a bassline.

'Slow. It's really slow. It must be peaceful in there.'

She climbs into the bed and leaves the duvet open like a door. Like the night before and the time before that, she waits and watches as you strip off any inhibitions at this midnight hour. You go to clamber in beside her and she shakes her head.

'Light. Please.'

Before you flick off the lamp, your eyes meet in the silence. The gaze requires no words at all. It is an honest meeting.

'Goodnight,' she says.

'Goodnight.' And for a moment, you surface from the fever dream, only to plunge once more.

Tonight is different, but the same. She slides a leg in between yours and pulls herself close and her deep breaths soften and round. You feel your body begin to slacken and sink towards sleep when she slips her leg out, turns away from you. You lie on your back facing the unmoving blackness of her ceiling when you feel her hand tapping against you.

'You OK?'

'Arm,' she says.

'Huh.'

'Arm.'

The arm which isn't trapped between her body and yours stretches towards her, and she pulls it across her body like a blanket, curling in tight. With her foot, she traces lines across your own, finally settling her lower limb between your calves. She slides down her bed a little, so she can tuck herself in the space between your chest and your chin, the mane of soft curls ticklish against your neck. You fit together, like this is an everyday. The hand holding your arm reaches for your own, spreading your digits between hers. Locking in. Tonight is different, but the same. Under what conditions does the uncontainable stay contained? Things unsaid don't often remain so. They take shape and form in ways one doesn't expect, manifesting in touches, glances, gazes, sighs. All you have wanted to do was hold each other in the darkness. Now, you have opened the box and left it unguarded in the night. You have both placed faith in the other that you will wake up intact. You have acted on a feeling. You are in a memory of the present. You are tumbling through a fever dream, surfacing only to plunge once more.

12

You would like to talk about the suppressions.

You are walking along Battersea Bridge. Leaning over the edge, the water choppy, the phone line clear, the words urgent, the language flimsy and insufficient, the feelings honest. You're standing on Battersea Bridge, watching the water ripple, and you wonder what caused the first ripple in this situation. She's at the airport, waiting for her flight to Dublin, asking the same question, retracing to the first night you met. She's trying to understand what passed between you that night, and simultaneously understanding that she cannot comprehend. She's thinking about your drunken excursion, from central to south-east London. More immediately, the five-day stretch in which you have barely left each other, in which nothing really happened but two friends sharing a bed and knowing an intimacy some never will. That is to ask, what is a joint? What is a fracture? What is a break?

'We're going round in circles at this point.'

'OK, well shit, lay it on me,' she says.

'We both know that something has happened in the past few days, something we can't ignore.'

'Nothing happened.'

'But that's the point. It would've been easier if we'd slept with each other. What happened was, I dunno. A bit more real.'

Her breath is thick as the silence down the line.

'So what do we do now?'

'I am running from this.'

'What does that mean?'

'I can't do this. There's too many factors, there's too much on the line. You're my friend. You're one of my closest. And my ex? Samuel would have a field day with this. Nah, this is too complex.'

'What about you? What do you want to do?'

'I have to go catch my plane.'

★

The next day, you can barely hear her on the phone over the clatter of cups in the café. You take refuge on the street, pacing in the small patch in front of the shop. Brick Lane is quiet, even for a weekday. You're wearing a T-shirt because spring is showing flashes of summer, cloudless blue, orange corona high in the sky. You're laughing and joking, and it's easier to do this, to open a box and close it quick, seal it with sharp quips, that is, until –

'I cannot wait to break this dry patch, you know.'

'Uh-huh.'

'Hoping you break yours soon too.'

'Oh. Erm.' She sniffs. 'Yeah, it's a little late for that.'

'Sorry?'

'I, er, yeah. I broke mine already.'

'But you only went back yesterday?'

'Yeah. It happened yesterday.'

'Oh. OK.'

'Are you all right?'

'Yeah,' you lie. 'I'm OK.'

'This is weird.'

'It is.'

'But it's not like I owe you anything. We're just friends.'

'You don't. We are.'

'I think I should go.'

'OK.' And she hesitates for a moment before signing off and hanging up.

You stand for some time, an unmoving car ploughed into from behind.

The same day, you leave an Uber – the walk from the station to your friend's house was too far in the darkness that fell quick and full. You have taken two or three steps. Your friend's house is in sight. You could throw a stone and it would shatter the window. You're thinking of an evening with a glass of wine, a record spinning in the background. You're thinking of good food and better company. You're in a memory of something yet to happen, when they stop you, like a moving vehicle edged off the road. They tell you there has been a spate of robberies in the area. They say many residents describe a man fitting your description. They ask where you are going and where you have come from. They say you appeared out of nowhere. Like magic, almost. They don't hear your protests. They don't hear your voice. They don't hear you. They don't see you. They see someone, but that person is not you. They would like to see what is in your bag. Your possessions are scattered across the ground in front of you. They say they are just doing their jobs. They say you are free to go now.

You make it halfway up the path to the door. You are hollowed out, like it was not just your bag they emptied. You are no longer in control of your limbs. You don't know how long you've been standing in front of the door when your friend calls, asking where you are. You tell them something has come up, that you won't be able to make it. You call an Uber and go home.

You tell no one about that incident, like you told no one about the time they stopped you, hard. Your friend was driving, one hand on the steering wheel, the other gesticulating as he preached. You remember talking about having faith and God and beauty and that which cannot be explained. You remember speaking of religion and power and Blackness. You remember making a joke which prised open his serious features, laughter

58

rumbling from his chest. You don't remember the contents of the joke, but you're sure, like much of your humour, it was quick, sharp, rooted in all you can explain and all you cannot. You remember the silence was heavy with all that was not said, all that goes unsaid. The moment stretched and held, and you knew both of you wanted to say you were scared and heavy, but reticence was a song you both knew by heart. Instead, you said you were hungry. He pulled over and that's when you heard a screech-squeal-scream of tyre.

Second time this week. Don't you get tired?

Drowned by screech-squeal-scream of get out of the car get out of the car get out of the car. They ordered you to the ground for symbolic purposes. Playing dead. You let out a skinny whimper sharp as a butter knife. You heard the sound rattle in your chest, pressing shut unserious features. Total eclipse. When you came to, you were beside yourself. This is what it means to die, you thought. Total eclipse. The sky turned black. Ha. You looked in one of their eyes and saw the image of the Devil. He had an index finger gripping the trigger, like he was holding onto a lifeline. He looked scared, behind the crumpled forehead, the hard eyes, he looked scared. He looked scared of what he did not know, of what was different. He looked scared because instead of questioning himself, of interrogating his beliefs, of not filling in the gaps, he continues to look at you as a danger. You fit the profile. You fit the description. You don't fit in the box but he has squeezed you in. He looked scared. They all did. You wouldn't accept their apologies, nor their extended hands, because even these are weapons in the darkness. Easy mistake to make. Second time this week for your friend, playing dead. Let's ask anyone else who has ever fit a description: you ever had to play dead? Have you ever not been seen? Are you tired?

But when it happens to you for a second time that week, you have to tell someone, even if it is yourself:

59

I was just walking home. Usual route, cut through the park. I'm what, thirty seconds away? If that. There's a car stopped at the intersection. It's weird, cause it's late, pitch-black out, the headlights are off, but the car isn't parked, there's a driver and a passenger. It's only when I really squint that the headlights flick on, full beam. Blinding. And then the car comes towards me, real slow, snail's pace, man. I could jog faster. Anyway, I start moving faster, but I know the car is gonna reach me before I get to my door. And when it does, the driver winds down the window, but doesn't say anything to me, neither of them do, just drive by real slow. It's weird, I didn't even notice the police markings on the car until they had pulled away.

It has only been a week since she called you and suggested that when you disembark from the DLR, you get an Uber to her house. You have spent the time tumbling. Today, on Saturday, you wake late in the morning. Your mother and father are already awake. It has not been long since they returned from Ghana. Something is not right. You can feel it. You enter their room, and your father is sitting on the edge of his bed. His shoulders have slumped inwards. He has slumped in on himself. A stale trail of tears runs down his cheeks. You pull him up and hold him close, letting him breathe in the comfort of your arms.

'Your grandfather is dead,' he whispers.

Grief rattles about your mind like a loose pebble in a shoe. You can't see where you're going. You call her. Despite everything, you call her, your closest friend, tell her that you're tired, in your spirit, that you have made peace with dying but it hurts all the same. And she sits on the phone while you weep, remains on the phone in silence when the tears have stopped, distracts you with her raucous humour, and when the conversation has run its course she reminds you that she's there, always there for you.

But even here, you are hiding. You cannot tell her about when your father walked into your room one evening, holding out the tiny black phone he uses for international calls.

'It's Grandad.'

Your body stiffened. The phone was still there, in your father's hand, the static on the line audible from a distance. You know of the man on the other end of the line: you speak a few times a year, ask each other customary questions about your lives, your health, but custom is where it stops. He is family, yes, but you don't know him. You take the phone to your room.

'Hello.'

'Oh. You don't call me?'

'Pardon?'

'You don't call me. I never hear from you. I don't have long left. You have to call me more often. I could go any day now.'

'OK,' you said and, dashing out of your room, returned the phone to your father.

Coming back to your room, the shame you were experiencing gained distinction. He was right. You didn't call him. He was in his eighties and, after several strokes, required assistance to live.

In your kitchen, you wonder what your tears are for: the loss of him or the loss of yourself?

To be you is to apologize and often that apology comes in the form of suppression. That suppression is indiscriminate. That suppression knows not when it will spill.

What you're trying to say is that it's easier for you to hide in your own darkness, than emerge cloaked in your own vulnerability. Not better, but easier. However, the longer you hold it in, the more likely you are to suffocate.

At some point, you must breathe.

13

Several months after the fever breaks, you are walking from your house in Bellingham to your friend Imogen's place in Gipsy Hill. It's May now. You see an extension cord trailing in the grass like a loose thought as a woman slices a blade through overgrown hedges. A man walking past, coming downhill, carrying his daughter. Tiny gold hoops in her ears. She grips on his shoulder, straddling either side of his torso; his arms around her waist. Sunlight chasing them down the hill. You walk on.

In her garden, you sit with the family. Two brothers, her father, Imogen. Her older brother fetches you a beer, the neck perspiring. You unpluck a button on your shirt, feeling a few beads of sweat release themselves from where they were trapped between material and skin. You all sit, basking in the first hints of summer sunshine, the lazier heat which rests and doesn't shift. Time slurs. You're holding an empty beer and Imogen is slurping at the dredges in her glass.

'Let's take refuge,' she says.

Indoors, you and your oldest friend share a sofa. Imogen tucks herself close and it's not unfamiliar. When you were at school, it would be she, waiting, patient, legs crossed, neck boughed over her phone display, when you emerged from basketball training in the evening. She would catch sight of you with her kind, attentive gaze and already be in motion.

'Good session?'

Murmured, breathless answer, growing into something coherent, finding form. Walking towards the enormity of the fields. Covering the circumference with a slow, measured trudge, once, twice. Time losing shape, dragged back by your parents wondering where you are. Departing from one another, tucking her tiny frame into your chest; declining the lift, wanting to walk, to carve out something coherent, to find a form.

On the sofa, she studies you with the same attentive gaze.

'What's going on in there?' she asks.

'I don't know if I should go meet my friend.'

'Why?'

'I just have a bad feeling.'

'Then don't go.'

'But I want to see her. She's only back from Dublin for a few days.'

'Just go with your instincts.'

You're not a prophet but you should trust yourself more often.

You leave Imogen, take the number 3 bus snaking down to Brixton, where you meet her and the poet. It's like the fever had never broken, it's like you have returned to that evening where you shared a table at dinner, the three of you. As before, when you're departing, the poet who sees you and her, saw the ripple and the sinking stone, tells both of you to stay out of trouble.

From Brixton Nando's to the Ritzy Cinema. To the bar. You order a whisky and she pulls a face. She, a sweet cider. There's a balcony, where you sit at a wobbly table and drink quickly, lest they spill. You're set back from the edge so it's screaming you hear first, followed by the smashing of glass, accusations being thrown, an anger, a hysteria. Feelings are heightened in these moments. You peer over the balcony, joining in with the rest of Brixton to view too many policemen for one woman. A knee on the woman's back. The small crowd on the balcony weigh in with their own heavy conclusions or, in one case, despair at their own hopelessness.

'I just wish there was something I could do.'

A stranger consoles another stranger. 'You can't. People like that, people who have been in Brixton for years, they're a lost cause.'

And you feel anger, a hysteria, feelings heightened in these moments, but your vision is clear, an unfrosted window, you see the woman with the policeman's knee on her back not being seen.

'Are you OK?' she asks. You shake your head.

'Finish your drink, let's go.'

You walk through Brixton, passing a Caribbean fete. Eyes follow her loose languid figure. When she gets into stride and a smile cracks open her features, you wonder if what people see matches what is. You suspect it does. You had that drink too quickly, you realize, but you don't think as you both walk into a Sainsbury's, and buy a bottle to split, both drinking too quickly, both drunk too quickly. Spillages. Spillages on the bus. Spillages on the path to her flat, where you both pause to question each other, but gloss over. It's easier this way, for now.

'I heard you bumped into Samuel.'

You hesitate. 'Who did you hear that from?'

'Samuel. I saw him yesterday, both got off at the same station.'

'Oh.'

'He asked me if anything was going on with us. I couldn't give him a straight answer.'

Neither could you. You had met Samuel in a similar fashion the week before, alighting from a train at Elephant and Castle, meeting on a platform. It was the first time in several months you had seen each other, and he was short, sharp, curt with you, before getting to the point.

'Are you and her together yet, then?'

'Who?'

'Don't treat me like an idiot,' Samuel said.

'We're not together.'

'But you want to be?'

'Where is this coming from?'

'I said, don't treat me like an *idiot*. I saw the way you looked at her when you first met. I saw the same look when I came over to hers that time, in December. I heard how you spoke about each other. It's whatever, bruv. You'll probably end up getting married. You're both adults, but shit, be honest about it. I'm tired of people lying to me. It's bad enough having to watch two people you care about fall for each other. But to not say anything? That's rubbish. So tell me what the deal is?'

'Honestly,' you said. 'I don't know.'

Except you did know. To give desire a voice is to give it a body through which to breathe and live. It is to admit and submit to something which is on the outer limits of your understanding. To have admitted it to Samuel would have unfurled the folds of longing which he witnessed the beginning of. To have admitted it to Samuel would have been asking him to renounce you of your guilt. It would have let the resistance fall away and given you the freedom to act. It was easier for you to remain silent and hold the desire to yourself. Samuel waited expectantly, waited for more, and when it wouldn't come, walked away from you.

As you walk the path to her flat, wobbly, drunk, you ask, 'Are you mad I didn't say anything?'

She shakes her head. 'Not really.'

'So you are.'

She smiles. 'When he told me, it felt weird. Felt like you were just looking out for yourself. I know it was just a chance meeting, but still.'

'Sorry.'

'Just tell me next time,' she says, winding an arm around your waist. 'Man, I've missed you.'

'Me too,' you say. 'Me too.'

★

Inside, you're sitting across the room. You're both talking to a young man lodging in her flat, aware that the third addition warps the dynamic. She nudges you with her eyes, and gestures at the empty spot in front of her. Why are you over there? she's saying. Come. So you go. Perch on a bare patch of carpet where her legs are trailing and lay your hand on her bare skin. Is this OK? you ask. It is, she says, it is, and so you're here, you're drunk, there's already been a spillage but you mopped it up. She runs a hand over your shorn head, tracing lines. The conversation moves, flows, swoops, boughs, but when he retires to bed, it's evident you've been waiting to be alone.

'You can't stay today. The lodger is staying in my room, I gotta sleep with my mum.'

'I know.'

She twists round and invites you to the sofa, invites herself to lay her head in your lap.

'Don't let me fall asleep here.'

Another change of position: she flips her body, so her legs are stretched across your lap, and props her head up on a pillow on the sofa.

'I have to go to bed soon,' she says.

And another: she sits up and curls her arms around you, kissing the material over your chest, kissing the exposed skin on your cheek, and you lean in, as does she, but she makes a diversion, and it's lips grazing cheek once more, and again. You lean closer, brushing her nose, but it's the same; she mirrors, and somewhere en route, a moment of resistance, or perhaps she is experiencing lucidity in her own mist. You play this game with each other, in which the stakes are far too high, on the sofa, in her kitchen, in her hallway; you wanting to make a journey, she wanting to do the same but making a diversion before the destination.

'Hey. Are you OK?'

66

She nods, separating your tangled limbs. 'I think you should go home.'

You walk home from Deptford to Bellingham. You spend the hour wondering about how you will both recollect this evening. You think about what it means to desire your best friend in this way. You think about holding onto this feeling for so long, holding it down, holding it in, because sometimes it's easier to hide in your own darkness than to emerge, naked and vulnerable, blinking in your own light. You think about whether she has been doing the same. You think about spillage, and whether this is something that can be mopped up. You think as you walk through the night, wandering familiar streets with these unfamiliar feelings. At some point, the sun begins to break the horizon, and you find yourself in the park, prone on the ground. The grass cool against the heat of your desire, life still against the pace of your racing heart.

14

It's summer now. You're working in NikeTown, on Oxford Circus, supplementing your money from photography. It started as a temporary gig, the year before last, meant as a stopgap after graduation. Now, it is a permanent fixture, and you're clocking in to clock out. You're clocking in and dreaming your days away. You're not entirely unhappy here, but herein lies the issue; this job is far too comfortable, and for the most part, considering you and your colleagues are cogs in a giant machine, you're all treated quite well.

The air conditioning has broken. The enormous windows have been designed to let as much daylight seep in as possible, giving the illusion that one is shopping outside, rather than in walled confines. You're daydreaming, thinking of spending your days elsewhere. You want to take a plane somewhere, and walk. The previous summer, you did just this, flying to Seville in August, where the heat clutches your whole being, tighter as the day goes on, relenting its grip only after siesta. You would wake early, and walk down to the restaurant underneath the apartment you were staying in, where, despite a decent grip of the language, you would muddle through a bleary-eyed conversation, ordering a *tostada* and a black coffee. The morning would be spent exploring the outer edges of the city, before returning to your apartment for a nap. You would wake and perch at the tiny desk in your room, writing by hand in a battered black notebook, opening the doors of your balcony wide and letting stray chatter drift towards you in many languages. You might have a snack, and walk some more, turning towards the heart of the city, going to a bar, later, sitting to eat tapas in a restaurant. From here, you would dangle your legs over the edge of the River Guadalquivir, the bank unprotected, one able to take a dip if one so wished. Many others had the same idea – the dangling rather than swimming in the river – a line of kicking legs, listening to the quiet swish of water lapping back and forth.

It's summer now, and you're craving a simpler existence. You want to read. You want to write. You want to meet strangers for dinner, and not refuse another drink at another bar. You want to dance. You want to find yourself in a basement, neck loose, bobbing your head as a group of musicians play, not because they should, but because they must. It's summer now, and you're looking forward to worrying less. You're looking forward to longer nights and shorter days. You're looking forward to gathering in back gardens and watching meat sputter on an open barbecue. You're looking forward to laughing so hard your chest hurts and you feel light-headed. You're looking forward to the safety in pleasure. You're looking forward to forgetting, albeit briefly, the existential dread which plagues you, which tightens your chest, which pains your left side. You're looking forward to forgetting that, leaving the house, you might not return intact. You're looking forward to freedom, even if it is short, even if it might not last.

You're looking forward.

It's summer now. You're working. You catch a glimpse of someone else's rhythm, and think, I know that song. The timeline equates – the academic year is finished, so she must be back in London – but it doesn't make you any less surprised. It is no less surprising when you find yourself taking long strides across the shop floor, moving at pace. Her hair is shorter, the curls tight and cropped, but everything else remains the same, her face full of joyous mischief, eyes alight with the sheen of laughter, her long body moving with a clumsy grace she has made her own.

As you take her into your arms, holding tight, pulling tighter, you realize the warmth between you remains.

'What are you doing here?' you ask.

'Hello to you too.'

'Yes, yes, hello, hi – you're back?'

'I am.'

'When, how, what?'

She's grinning at you, watching your excitement spill over into nervous babble.

'Come here,' she says, pulling you into an embrace once more.

'How long has it been? A month?'

She nods. 'About that.' A pause. 'Too long. Much too long.'

You separate and she reaches for your face, but doesn't quite make contact, tracing your outline, giving you form and detail. It's summer now, and she's drawn a line towards you, or maybe the line always existed, will always exist. It's summer now, and language is still flimsy, inadequate, so you stand, silenced by the weight of it all, letting your bodies confess their truths.

It's summer now, so you're all moving slower. DJ Screw, legendary Houston pioneer of chopped and screwed music, would make songs *at slower tempos, to feel the music and so you can hear what the rapper is saying. I make my tapes so that everyone can feel them.* For Screw, slowing a record down allowed it to breathe.

There is a pleasurable freedom in this slowness; where the frequencies lower and it is not so much a matter of the head but the chest. You say words with your chest. You feel bass slap thud, like a heartbeat. You say words with your chest and know there is power in your voice. You say words with your chest and trust yourself. You speak and realize that, in slowing down to speak, you can breathe. It's a strange turn of phrase, you think, being allowed to breathe, having to seek permission for something so natural, the basis of life; in turn, having to seek permission to live.

It's summer now, so let's slow down, and breathe. Let's say you're playing basketball on Saturday afternoon in July, and you're sprawled out on the sideline, taking a breather. You reach into your bag and pull out the bulk of your 35mm film camera, always heavy in the hand. You start to take photos, and later, when you've dipped the negatives in chemicals, you see you took one by accident. Your finger depressed the shutter a split second after taking one before. It was sunny, so maybe 1/250 of a second after, and later, once you've developed the film, this is what came out:

The ball has left the shooter's hand. It's spinning backwards as it moves through the air. All four players of this game of two on two cease motion to watch a ball rotate through the air at a rate quicker than the eye can acknowledge. The shooter wills the ball towards the hoop. The others have their own intentions, but the shooter, you know, he wants the ball to go in. The sky is blue and there's a dusting of cloud. It's twenty-six degrees on a Saturday afternoon in July. If the ball goes in, they will pick it up and start a new round from the top. If it does not, one or more of the players will rush towards the ball, and they will continue to play. They do this because they need to, they want to. They do this because they can feel it.

There's so much more you wish to say but there aren't the words.

It's summer now and language is flimsy but sometimes it is all you have. You're sitting in your garden, mouth prised open in this heat. On the small table in front of you, ice shrinks in water, and your notebook is as still as the air, humid and sticky. You're writing her letters, building her a world you can share. You're writing about seeing the hanging orb in the sky when one should not; the moon resting there, pale against the daylight, fleshy in the darkness. You're trying to write slow, so she can hear what you're saying, but also because there is pleasure in this, where it is not so much a matter of the head but of the chest.

Speaking of, A Tribe Called Quest is playing. *The Low End Theory*. You are wondering what led Q-Tip, unspoken bandleader, to carve away everything on the high end of sound, allowing the low end of sound, the bass, to dominate, allowing it to speak as if it was a prayer, a desire for freedom. This isn't an angry album. Sure, there are a plethora of characters who make an appearance, but they are there for purposes of visibility; the album is about being seen, about being heard; it is about freedom, even if it is brief, even if it is only to be found in a head nod on Phife's verse for 'Butter', even if it is only to be found in the joyful surprise for Busta Rhymes' scene-stealing verse on 'Scenario'. Hanif Abdurraqib wrote about this album, wondering how strange a life, to be presented to the world, through your flaws; through blood, swollen face, your bent body. How strange a life you and other Black people lead, forever seen and unseen, forever heard and silenced. And how strange a life it is to have to carve out small freedoms, to have to tell yourself that you can breathe. But how beautiful it is when those freedoms arrive, when you are breathing, when you're matching Phife word for word, or singing the refrain, *We got the jazz, we got the jazz*. How beautiful, when you're in a crowd, and you find your wandering gaze met by another, twenty, thirty metres away, both of you unaware that your shoulders and hips are moving to the bassline, because this is not something you have had to think about for once, this is something you just do, and understanding this, and the circumstances which brought you to this moment, you both raise a small hand of acknowledgement. How wonderful are moments like these, where you don't have to hide? How wonderful to realize, amidst thrum of a bass drum, that sometimes it is a joy to be alive?

It's summer now. You're outside, wearing shorts and a sleeveless jersey, and still sweat pours from your own pores. Through the solid wall of sound – from indoors, you've turned *The Low End Theory* on, loud – her voice drifts towards you. Your brother must have let her into the house – your parents are away once more, on a holiday back home this time, which makes the equation of you and her easier, without the pressure of an introduction. She comes from the house, into the garden, on the phone, smiling, listening as she does so well. She kisses you on the top of your head, and settles in the seat opposite you, pulling her culottes up past her knees.

'Hot,' she mouths.

You head into the kitchen and pour her a glass of water that's mostly ice. She's finishing up the phone call when you return.

'Hello, friend.'

'What's going on?' you say, setting the glass beside your own.

'Oh, nothing.' She raises her arms. 'It's summer now.'

'It is, indeed.'

It's summer now, so as you did in Seville before you met her, you spend the afternoon together outside, eating, drinking, before taking refuge in the house.

'I need to nap,' she says, the heat robbing her of the desire to do anything. The heat making you both slow, so slow you can hear each other, you can hear your prayers.

Your room has changed slightly since she was last here. You cleared most of the towers of books from your desk, now only a mountain on the left side of what you've read most recently, what you hope to read soon. There's a stack of records on the floor too; you have been trying your hand at sampling from vinyl, listening carefully for snatches of sound you can layer over each other to form new rhythms.

She sprawls out on your bed, atop the covers, then sits up suddenly to remove the large gold hoops swinging from her ears. You lie beside her, settle into a familiar position. The break since this last happened has made no difference. You fit, like this is an everyday. The only difference here is sunshine filtering through your light curtains. This is a daydream rather than a night-time reverie.

She pulls your arm close, tucking it towards her chest; you shift your hips closer, your chest pressed against her back. Her breathing quickens.

'You good?'

'I just had a weird moment,' she says, muffled, 'where I realized, if you wanted you could kill me in my sleep.' You cannot help but laugh.

'Not funny,' her voice trailing away.

'Don't worry. You're safe here.'

It's summer now, so you can sit on her balcony, drinking wine, sipping slow. You've hopped around London all day, going from your house, to the National Theatre on the Southbank, walking along the river as it lapped against its borders. You're back at her house now, talking into the night. You're talking about art and expression and suppression, and this is when you bring up the film *Moonlight*. You saw it first at a free screening in east London, and were struck by how a mood could be expressed through colour, the vivid palette Liberty City offers providing the backdrop for a story you began to increasingly feel in your chest. Blues and pinks and purples. When you left the cinema, you could not speak. When you rode the train home, you could not speak. You walked home, straight to your room. Silent tears fell like soft rainfall. You saw yourself in each version of Chiron. You saw yourself in the muting and erasure of his various expressions through the film. You saw yourself crumpling small to fit. You saw yourself when Juan says to Chiron: *Give me your head . . . let your head rest in my hands . . . I got you, I promise you. You feel that right there? You in the middle of the world, man.*

In the ebb and flow of the water, Chiron floats, then thrashes about with the support of his surrogate guardian. When the time comes, Juan lets him go; Chiron, head above the surface, eyes closed, mouth wide with the effort, swims, scooping water with each clumsy stroke. Juan's eager laughter fills your ears. He's doing it. Chiron is swimming. You felt bass slap thud, like a heartbeat, where Jidenna's 'Classic Man' is chopped and screwed, the phrases of music slowed, slow, slow, elongated vocals, lower frequencies, in your chest, it's in your chest. In the final scene, Chiron splits open like fresh fruit, tears running down his flesh.

Who is you?

I'm me, man. I ain't trying to be nothing else.

You were in your room, after the screening, sobbing silent, soft gasps, not because it pained you but because there was hope yet.

It's summer now. As she swirls her wine in her glass, she asks, 'Can you read to me? It's been a while since you read to me.'

The last piece you had read to her was about the previous summer, 2017, when you saw what happened when anger finally finds an escape, like a creeping wave finding form and crashing to shore. You began to write because photos have their own language, and sometimes, the images you make become flimsy in comparison to what you can feel. Sometimes, even this language fails. So you wrote your thoughts down, hoping to structure a narrative around the conflict bubbling inside you. You wish it were as straightforward as a random act of violence, but it was not. It was not that simple.

Let's home in for a moment, on the boy, who you glimpsed sitting on the wall, cuffed, surrounded by police officers. With his beautiful dreaded hair framing his face like open curtains, and how he wanted to be seen and heard, and what led him to want to be seen and heard. What led him here? What led him to outlet his anger into another? That anger which is the result of things unspoken from now and then, of unresolved grief, large and small, of others assuming that he, beautiful Black person in gorgeous Black body, was born violent and dangerous; this assumption, impossible to hide, manifesting in every word and glance and action, and every word and glance and action ingested and internalized, and it's unfair and unjust, this sort of death – being asked to live so constrained is a death of sorts – so you don't blame him for the anger, but why did his anger have to find a home in another who looked just like him?

Let's ask: which came first, the violence or the pain? This was more than you could comprehend, so you wrote the question down, inserted it at various points in the text, and hoped others would not ask why the boy with the beautiful dreads wielded sharp blade in dark hand, piercing Black skin; they would not ask why the event happened, but what the root was.

You read it to her, a few weeks after you met. It wasn't the first piece you read but it was more honest, it was more *you*. It was trauma, yes, but it was you and you were OK with her consuming it. You handed her the work and that was sufficient. You didn't need to explain to her that you felt joy too, that you were angry, you were scared, that walking home in the night worried you sometimes, because you didn't know which fate would meet you, the one who looked like you or the one who couldn't see you, or couldn't see you as you were meant to be seen, or whether you would arrive home without incident, and live to fear another day.

*

It's summer now. You have freedom in her presence and it means you don't have to hide. When your voice wavers, it is because you're struggling with the weight of the reality you speak of. Tucked together on her sofa, you read from a work in progress, this passage:

Policemen give each other a warning, like in this video, whereby on seeing an object in a young Black man's hand, one of a pair screams to the other, 'Gun, gun, gun!' before they both unload, twenty shots in all, four connecting with a body that is no longer his own, perhaps never was, after all, it's not a sudden loss of rights that enables a pair of men to destroy another's body on suspicion, no, it's not sudden; the perception of a young Black male existed long before this moment, before he fit a description, before two policemen and a helicopter deemed him to be the person smashing the windows of cars, despite not having proof, despite only being told 'someone' in the area was smashing the windows of cars, no, it's not sudden, this moment has been building for years, many years longer than any of these men have been alive, this moment is older than us all, it's longer than the 1:47 clip which shows me a murder –

She grips your foot with slender fingers, anchoring you in this moment as your voice falters and you begin to slip away. Just a few minutes ago, you had been seated on her balcony, the air cool as she smoked into the night, a slight flutter of her eyes with every inhale. She suggested you read to her. It had been a while. You pretended to deliberate, scrolling through the document on your phone, despite knowing where your finger would stop the page. You began to read in that clear voice which you think resembles an old friend telling you a story. You began to read and you were taken back to the moment the video appeared from across the Atlantic, transferred by the sturdy boat of the Internet. How his body crumpled, and he fell onto his hands and knees, as if crawling. When your voice wavers, it is because you're struggling with the weight of the reality you speak of. You're mad too, because policemen give each other a

77

warning, like in this video, whereby on seeing an object in a young Black man's hand, one of a pair screams to the other, 'Gun, gun, gun!' before they both unload, twenty shots in all. You're mad because Stephen and Alton and Michael and you, you too, received a warning but you didn't know where or when or how the danger would arrive. You just knew you were in danger.

You're not in danger here, but the tears fall all the same.

'Drunk,' you lie.

'It's OK. You're safe here.'

15

'Why did you ask me to hang out today?'

'That's a strange question to ask your friend,' you reply.

Golden hour swarms your senses. Colour tears through the sky in haphazard strokes. Your hand is bleeding and you're sucking the spillage from your thumb; you tried to open a bottle of cider with a key and the jagged edge sliced shallow through your skin. You've both been touched by the heat and the alcohol, but it makes this meeting no less honest.

'Usually, we just, you know, bump into each other or link up on the day. This felt kinda . . . formal?'

You shrug. 'I just wanted to carve out some time for you.'

'I appreciate that.' She takes a sip of her drink and comes up empty. 'Shall we get moving?'

When the day started, she was angry at you, and you didn't know why. You had an inkling and pushed apologies towards her in the way one would do when diffusing a bomb in the movies: one eye closed, snip at the wire and hope for the best.

She asked you to take her portrait. You placed her against the brickwork fencing her balcony and waited for both of you to relax. Your hands shook as she handed you her vulnerability, and you struggled to focus the lens on her features. When the contact sheet returns, the grid of pictures resembles a tussle; two people wrestling with how they feel about one another. The face does not lie. How the eyes widen, the skin around the mouth tightening, or, your favourite from the set, the last shot on the roll of film, where you trained the lens in her direction in a moment where her eyes were on you, not the lens, but you, and all guises slipped away with the ease of a gossamer sheet in the wind.

And as the sun set, you whispered secrets and intimacies into the solitude of the now empty sky. She asked you who you were –

'What a question,' you said.

'It's not that I don't know you, there are just bits and pieces that need filling in.'

You wonder what it means to know someone, and whether it's possible to do so wholly. You don't think so. But perhaps in the not knowing comes the knowing, born of an instinctive trust that you both struggle to elucidate or rationalize. It just is.

From south to north, mainline, Underground, emerging only to submerge. You enter a pub, and they direct you down the stairs, towards a bunker-like basement.

'What are you drinking?' you say.

'We are drinking . . . rum and Coke?'

'Single or double,' the woman behind the bar asks.

'Double,' she says.

The barwoman gazes at us, two giggly fools at ease, and takes comfort in our joy. The measures she pours are healthy, spilling over the limit, and she gives us a nod, a smile, a small acknowledgement. You look around the basement and remember that being seen is no small joy.

'I'm gonna go to the toilet before they start,' she says, heading round a corner.

As she leaves there's a crackle of feedback from the speakers. Your friend Theo takes the stage, his band quickly joining. He announces himself, and this is a different person from the young man you know. This is a person who is more certain, this is a person who is confident in his honesty. The songs are full of nostalgia, which is to say they are full of mourning; one remembers that which came before, often with a fond sadness, a want to return, despite knowing to return to a memory is to morph it, to warp it. Every time you remember something, the memory weakens, as you're remembering the last recollection, rather than the memory itself. Nothing can remain intact. Still, it does not stop you wanting, does not stop you longing.

She joins you halfway through the third song, and has ditched the patterned kimono she was wearing, now stuffed in her bag. A band of black cotton covers her chest, stomach and clean shoulders exposed. You hand her her drink and she leans back into you, the spread of brown skin pressed against your chest, meeting the slither of flesh where you have unbuttoned your shirt one more than usual. One arm snakes around her, your fingers perched on her collarbone. She eases into you further and you're in a rhythm, hips slinking slow, moving to memories of moments just passed. You are here and you are not. You are on the balcony, you are on the hill, you are in sunshine, you are in darkness, you are in the open air, you are in the basement, you are in perpetual joy, you are eternally sad. Her short black curls tickle your chin as her head winds this way and that. You wonder how long this moment could stretch for, and how much it could contain: you, her, this crowded basement of singles and couples and groups, the Black woman at the bar who *sees* you both, who you see too, Theo and his band on stage, nostalgia, melancholy, joy, concrete floors, makeshift walls, applause, a night too warm, introductions, cigarette split, eyes narrow, nicotine, one more drink, one more drink, one more drink –

And you're on a sofa in the pub, sticky leather on skin. Nursing what will be your last, she sits beside you, cross-legged, your hand resting against the ridges of her spine.

'That's not a platonic hand on my back,' she says.

'Oh, my bad,' you say.

'No, it's OK. I like it.'

★

81

Maybe it's because you need to make the journey back to south-east London, maybe it's because you're both running out of steam. It could also be that, despite interacting with others, this has been largely an experience shared between the two of you, and a new venue might change these conditions, might cause the thing you are both holding onto to end.

'Honestly,' you say, just before your friends dive into another basement, a small group of you having walked from Stoke Newington to Dalston. 'I think we're done for tonight. Go enjoy yourselves.'

They don't need to be told. You split away, considering a taxi.

'Let's get some food,' she says to you.

The chicken shop you choose is cosy, yet sterile, the light harsh. They have opened their glass front, which is a set of enormous sliding doors, the night coming in with no filter.

'What do you want?' she asks.

'Wings and chips. Please.' She smiles, and orders the same, handing over a plastic note. You hold her close, to say thank you, and she lets lips she had painted purple graze your cheek.

'Do you wanna eat on the way home,' she says, squirting chilli sauce over her chips, 'or sit in here?' She fans herself, batting away the idea as she says it.

'It'll be cooler outside. Let's find a bench or something, I'll order an Uber when we're done.'

The place you perch ends up being the cool concrete of someone's stairs. You point to a building opposite and tell her how, many years ago, a diminutive, softly-spoken man spoke his joy in a basement full of strangers, playing long-forgotten cuts and songs you grew up with. You tell her this but soon you have trailed off, tearing into the chicken, dashing the bones away into the gutter. Something heavy here, in the absence of your words.

You feel her turn beside you. You wonder how long this moment could stretch for, and how much it could contain: you,

her, the soft rush of cars speeding in the darkness, the gaze, seeing each other here, her heartbeat near audible, before she says,
'I love you, you know?'

She has swum out into open water, and it is not long before
you join her.

You take but a moment before saying, 'I love you too.'

16

She makes you sleep on the sofa, and you're glad because, in the taxi home, as she was leaning out of the window, you realized it was alcohol you were swimming in, not water.

It's better it happens this way.

Sunday evening. She asked if you wanted to go to the cinema in the afternoon, Peckhamplex, five-pound tickets and the promise of audience participation, but at the last moment had broken your date to see her family. Instead, an evening where she pants with the heat, on her sofa, watching reality TV.

'I'm so full and hot,' she says.

And here, another problem: despite advocating for desire to bloom in the summer, the rays of the sun falling on faces, skin darker and full of life, gentle smiles for no reason but the sunshine, despite all this, one often finds oneself reduced to sludge when you haven't eaten enough or eaten too much, dehydrated or had one too many, dropping off for unplanned naps or sleep deprived in the thick nights. None of which is conducive to being in the presence of others, yet you soldier on, you are determined to enjoy these months, leaving the house not knowing what the day might bring you, where possibilities seem infinite, where beauty and joy, too, can be endless.

You while away the evening together, doing nothing really, which is something, is an intimacy in itself. To not fill your time with someone is to trust, and to trust is to love. And so you should say you spent the evening loving each other, on her sofa, eating, drinking, listening to music. She plays Kendrick, and you talk about that for a moment. But even this trails away, content in the absence of distractions, content in the presence of one another.

It's better it happens this way: that you have no intention of it happening. The time approaches for you to leave, but it's Sunday and the buses have stopped running. You have work in six hours. You should've left long ago. But you're here, in the dim darkness of her room, the night not quite black, some light seeping under the curtains. She welcomes you into her room, and asks you to close the door. Asks you to turn around so she can change her T-shirt. To trust is to love and she trusts you. Asks how you're gonna get home. An Uber, you guess. You check how long it will take. Ten minutes. You had no intention of this happening. But you don't decline when she asks if you'd like to lie beside her and wait. You don't edge away when she pulls closer. Your breathing weighs more here. She swims out into the open water and you join her. You're here, tucked together, her back against your chest. It's familiar, even when you reach under her shirt, and take a nipple, tender, between forefinger and thumb, the rest of your hand splayed against her warm skin. Your breathing weighs more here. Your Uber comes, your Uber goes. You hear your phone vibrating, the driver trying to find you, but you don't pick up. Your lips are grazing her neck, and one arm is pinned between you and her, but the other, the other wanders, wanders down, down, down, a finger grazing her stomach, grazing the delicate curves of her hips and waist, grazing the black material which separates you from her, before you become surer, a little more firm. You don't know if what you feel is a result of the heat or the heat breaking between you. What is a break? What is a fracture? What is a joint? To love is to trust, and she trusts your hand to break the thin wall, sliding your hand under the material. Your lips meet and it's urgent. Your lips meet and you know you have needed to kiss her. You turn her on her back, your mouth now finding her stomach, working upwards to where your hand previously was, to what started this all, but no, she started this all, when she suggested you get an Uber to her house, but no, you don't know; you don't know where her roots lie but you can certainly trace yours to the dingy pub in which you met this woman with braids coming down her head, a kind-eyed stranger, and you knew before you knew. Is this OK? you ask, hooking the black material separating you from her with your thumbs. She nods, you slide it down, down, down. Away. There is no wall to break now but there is more to explore and you know, you know what you're doing, but only because it is her, only because you can feel her body tighten as you touch her, only because you had no intention of this happening, and so you're not thinking, but feeling, and you're not talking but your bodies are confessing their truths out loud. You run your tongue down her middle, from the hard bone of her chest, down her stomach, down, down, down. She stops you. Are you sure? she asks. You nod in the darkness and continue, your tongue meet-ing soft flesh, slow and steady, her body writhing in your presence, in the pleasure. She asks you to come back to her, so you lie beside her. Your lips meet, urgent. Lie on your back, she says. And she kisses you, working from your mouth, to your neck, the hardness of your collarbone, the softness of the skin on your chest, working down, down, down, down the middle. It's not long before you're giggling as you fumble in the dark with your best friend. She lies beside you once more and amidst the laughter, a short panic, which you thrust away in bursts, kissing the darkness, pushing each other, lips meeting, urgent. The heat has broken, and you know what you feel is the result. You're swimming with her, holding hands in the dark with your best friend, taking large, sure strokes. You had no intention of this happening, but it's better this way.

17

She spends the week apartment hunting in Dublin. She's left it late; only a few weeks of the summer remain. You don't talk about what happened, not really. But what more is to be said that your bodies did not? You do however, from a distance, fall into a rhythm like it is easy.

On her return, you're waiting at the airport, sat atop the empty help desk. Legs swinging like a joyous child. She strides through the evening, and she waves. You wave back, your heart swelling at this small gesture.

You said to trust is not to fill time, but you would like to say to trust is to fill that time with each other. The heart does the same, in the immense darkness of the body, filling with blood, clenching it out, tight as stiff fist with nothing in hand. You fill time, clutching onto it as it leaves you. Clutching after each other in the moments you must separate. In between the weekly shops, the mind-numbing television, cooking, cleaning, reading. Perched separately, but together, you often find yourself close to the balcony as it rains, heat breaking in thunder and lightning, like snare hits and hi-hats.

You're like a pair of jazz musicians, forever improvising. Or perhaps you are not musicians, but your love manifests in the music. Sometimes, your head tucked into her neck, you can feel her heartbeat thudding like a kick drum. Your smile a grand piano, the glint in her eye like the twinkle of hands caressing ivory keys. The rhythmic strum of a double bass the inert grace she has been blessed with, moving her body in ways which astound. A pair of soloists in conversations so harmonious, one struggles to separate. You are not the musicians but the music.

18

It's one thing to be looked at, and another to be seen.

'Can I?' you ask, holding up your camera. You spend a lot of time gazing through a viewfinder, in what you think of as a perfect position: the objective observer, perched in the near distance, straddling the fence between here and there. The subject is aware but not distracted from themselves. Perhaps the observer will ask the subject to turn this way or that, will ask them to show them something else – not more or less, but different. The subject acquiesces – the resistance is natural. There's an inter-action of sorts, between the pair, and this makes the portrait. The photo you're thinking of: she gazes straight into the lens, as you've asked. Holding her neck for comfort. Single silver earring swinging soft from the lobe. She's beautiful – subjective, but the bias is inevitable. The glint in her eyes you are always searching for before you depress the shutter. A moment cut from some-thing you both struggle to describe. Something like freedom.

In a conversation with a friend:
    'I'm about to nerd out so forgive me – so my biggest influence is this British-Ghanaian painter Lynette Yiadom-Boakye, her work is dope. She paints Black figures, but all of them are made up – which when you see the detail of them is hard to believe. By doing this, she's externalizing her interiority, which isn't some-thing Black people are afforded very often. At the same time, her level of craft is nuts – there's a lot of power in mastery of a form, being able to flex within that. Then with the motion stuff, I guess I'm always trying to make things which are reflective of

Black music, which, to me, is some of the greatest expression of Blackness – that ability to capture and portray a rhythm. So maybe *motion* is the wrong word, *rhythm* is better. So like this shot of her holding her face, there's a lot of stillness to it but there's also a peaceful rhythm in that moment captured.'

A few months before, you had attended a talk on an exhibition of Sola Olulode's work, in a gallery in Brixton. Her paintings were expressions of joy. Blue canvases, the bodies moving freely in celebration of life. Even in the silence of a canvas, the beat is loud and physical, channelled through her subjects, the Black woman centralized in her work. Aside from the feelings the work evokes, her craft is extraordinary. The brushwork! You haven't seen such attention to craft since Lynette –

But you'd hate to conflate, so you stay silent. It's enough to be in this room, in this space, where those who are usually looked at, and objectified, are seen, heard; can live, laugh, breathe.

When the talk was over, you took the time to speak to both artwork and artist, marvelling at the figures struggling to be contained on the canvas, your eyes dancing across the cloth she has taken so much time and care with. You thanked her for the work and watched a sly smile spread across the face of a woman who was still wondering if she was supposed to be here, is yet to convince herself.

Still, as you parted ways, you wondered if you're wrong, if freedom isn't as full as you imagine – no, if freedom is not an absolute – no, try again – if freedom is something one could always feel. Or if you are destined to feel it in small moments here and there.

It's one thing to be looked at and another to be seen. You're asking to see her as you take her portrait, hurtling through south-east London. There, as a solid shaft of amber light breaks through the glass, grazing cheeks, lips, eyes, the eyes themselves like light diffracted through infinite glass; you see hazel, green, yellow; you see a trust you are grateful for. The mechanism in your camera snaps shut as your finger touches the trigger. Her face on celluloid, development pending.

You follow each other around the supermarket, searching for snacks you know won't sate your hunger. Down an escalator, exchanging nothings as you avoid the impending split, she heading to north London, to a house party, you south, to meet friends. On the concourse, you press her cheek against yours, wrap arms around a lithe body you have grown to know, the small moans of reluctance slipping from your mouths not enough to convey what you are feeling. Not that words are ever enough.

You're on the phone to her on the other ends of your Tube journeys. She stays on while you foolishly decide to walk through the forest in this furthermost corner of south London, the trees like gnarled arms stretching skyward on either side. As you emerge into a clearing, she says she wrote something about you on the train. Your chest tightens, like the hands of the forest are clutching your torso. You speak a little more as you walk her to her party – strange that your voices soundtrack so much of each other's lives, but it feels right, you wouldn't pick another – and, finding someone to let her in, her voice leaves you, but when she hangs up, it's as if her hand is still in yours, long fingers interlocked, her thumb caressing the flesh below your wrist. Every few moments, you check your phone, only to be rewarded with a blank screen. You're, as always, thinking of her. You wonder if she's decided against sending it. You wonder if she's taken back her words, only to leave you with what could be. You wonder as you wander, taking in a view from the clearing akin to that from her balcony, wide and sweeping, looking out across the city. Then, like when you are tangled on her sofa watching red lights flicker across London's skyline, she gives your hand a little squeeze. You check your phone once more and see her name on the screen.

On the parched patch of grass, you stand still, stunned. Read her words once, twice, hearing the sweetness in her voice with each turn of phrase. You lock yourself in the toilet when you arrive and take them in once more, letting the sentences caress your scalp. Think of this: she closes her eyes and prises open your chest, one rib at a time – she knows what to do, she doesn't need to see – slipping her sentences next to your beating heart, the small bundle of muscles swelling beneath her hand. A symptom of something which could only be known as joy.

'Are you two a thing now?'

The journey you have made is to an apartment your friend Abi and her boyfriend, Dylan, have rented for his birthday. They both live at home, so they wanted a little more space. You're early. It's just the three of you. More are on their way. Something slow, funky, with a heavy bassline spreads from the speaker into the living room. Night has fallen. Time has slowed, as has your rhythm.

'I guess,' you say.

'You guess?' Abi takes a sip of her wine. 'Don't be scared now.'

But you are. You haven't admitted it to anyone, perhaps this is the first time you've admitted it to yourself. You're scared of this moment, which feels like when you wandered onto the beach to photograph lightning in the middle of a storm, volatile and gorgeous, unpredictable strands falling haphazard from the sky. You didn't know what you would capture, and you knew it was a risk, but it was something you had to do. Here, you know that this is a feeling you cannot ignore.

It's one thing to be looked at, and another to be seen; you're scared that she might not just see your beauty, but your ugly too.

'Where is she?'

'At another party.'

'Is it far? Tell her to come.'

What if she says no?

'She's not going to say no.'

'Did I say that out loud?'

'You didn't have to. Call her.'

She picks up after a couple of rings and the party spills onto the line.

'Where are you?'

'I'm still at the party,' she says. 'Leaving soon, though.'

'I think you should get into an Uber and come here.'

'You think I should get an Uber and come to you?'

'Yes.'

There's a pause, and it's like everything has stopped. Even the party has lulled in the background.

'Send me the address.'

You're holding the camera once more. Her long frame curled up on the windowsill, puffing on a cigarette. You take the shot, and she takes the camera from you, places it on the side. Takes your hand instead. The warmth of her hand in yours, the thumb at work once more. She blinks, slowly, just before her lips stretch into a smile. She pulls you closer. She's swaying a little, and you realize she's leading you in a dance. The bassline is thicker, faster, but slow enough that this doesn't feel like a rush. Slow enough to gaze into her eyes as you press closer, moving in an easy, measured rhythm.

You're scared. But when you hear music, and something, something takes you, closes your eyes, moves your feet, hips, shoulders, bobs your head, reaches inwards, invites you to do the same, leads you, if only for a moment, towards something else which has no name, needs no name, do you question it? Or do you dance, even when you don't know the song?

19

Speaking of music and rhythms, it's Carnival Sunday and what should be dub shaking your bones is the muffled roar of rain. It comes as warned, steady and light. She had already made her decision to seek alternative arrangements, but it doesn't hurt to lament.

'The one day in the year when I just want to turn up, and dance, and have fun – and we get this,' she says, signalling the spit falling from the dirty grey sky. Thunder crackles, like the distant rumble of a giant's stomach, and she sighs, the short whoosh joining nature's sounds.

The night before, you had been sitting on her sofa, when she made the declaration.

'I don't think that's a good idea,' you said.

'Why not?'

'I just . . . it's quite sudden.'

'But I want to. Come on, come help me.'

In the bathroom, you laugh and giggle as she wets her hair, flattening the curls with water. You don a glove and help ease the dye across her soft scalp, once, twice, until the desired colour is reached. She is going from dark to blonde, spreading chemicals as one does in a darkroom, to encourage an image to emerge from celluloid. The beauty of shooting on film is in the unexpected. You don't know what will appear out of the development process. You are doing the same here, the bleach on her dark roots producing a glow like sunshine at golden hour. When you settle in bed for the night, you run your hand through her yellow curls, and she murmurs towards slumber.

'This feels good,' she says. 'This has felt good. I've enjoyed this summer together.'

'It's not over yet,' you say, but she's already asleep.

Carnival Sunday. Bits and pieces like a film strip: walking through puddles on Rye Lane, determined to find a space where she would feel safe. Peering into the barbershop, doing a *walk by*. Holding her by the underside of your forearms. It will be OK, you tell her, not because she's nervous, but because you believe it. Inside, waiting for a chair to become free. A measure of rum to ease the jitters. 'Is that your boyfriend?' The answer is too complex: when you have the words to explain, they will still feel inadequate. 'I won't hurt her,' the barber says, noticing how you eye him as the razor glides across her scalp. You hear the conversation and know she has found another place to feel comfortable. Two dots of blood on her forehead as he lines her up. You both promise to return. It doesn't feel empty.

Carnival Sunday. You're scraping the plate with your forks. Left-overs from the day before, rice and peas, jerk chicken, the meat slipping from the bone.

'I have to go soon,' you say. 'You still heading out?'

'I think so,' she says, suppressing a yawn. 'We're taking a nap,' she says, leaving the room.

In her bedroom, you clamber into bed, pull the duvet over yourself, suddenly tired.

'Wait,' she says.

'What?'

She giggles. 'Did you really think we were taking a nap?'

Carnival Sunday. You return later that night after leaving her house for a few hours. Kick off your shoes without undoing the laces. She's where you left her, in bed, the grin still traced on her lips, her words still echoing pleasantly, like laughter: 'Did you really think we would take a nap?'

It's night now, and the rain has stopped. You describe the party you left her for and wonder about the enormous street party you didn't make it to.

'There's always next year.'

She nods, settling into the folds of her duvet. You wrap your arms around her, letting them linger, comforted by her warmth. Her curves and juts are familiar. The shape of her recognizable, even with the newly cropped blonde hair. She smells like her, which is a cop-out, really, but if pushed, you would say she smells like a place you call home.

20

Miserly grey of a London sky on Carnival Monday. Hot and muggy and stiff. Summer's beginning to stall and dwindle. You ran into a friend at Victoria train station. You hadn't seen each other for years, not since way before he found his freedom being taken from him, but this isn't the time or place, no, this is a time for joy and so neither of you mention the letters you wrote to each other during his eighteen-month stint, neither of you joke about his slim frame gaining mass, neither of you suggest that there might be something else, something like tired, swimming in his dark brown eyes. You embrace and exchange numbers, promising to link up later in the day, both knowing the possibility of phone reception during Carnival is slim. You split, heading underground. When you emerge, London is still grey, the sky a single colour. As luck would have it, you bump into more friends trudging along the route, following sound and signs. *Heading towards a house party. Rooftop vibes, they've got a little balcony.* You're reminded of Leah and Michel taking up Frank's invitation to an *amazing carnival pad* in Zadie's NW.

You can see everything from here. No need to lumber through the mass of people searching for a toilet or chicken or avoiding noise and violence on the ground, there's always violence here, *I guess that's what you expect when* – yes? That's what you expect when? And in the silence, someone offers you a sausage roll and a Red Stripe and tells you to eat and drink until you are content. The room begins to spin in blue anger. There's mimicry of broken English, like patois was a luxury, rather than a necessity, like the language did not emerge from Black body being split. There's a Rasta wig here too. You are unsurprised that you don't have fun. No one notices you slip onto stairs onto street into Carnival, just in time to witness a crime being committed. Woman, bringing the yellow pastry of a patty towards her open mouth. Man, charges towards her with no regard, his elbow knocking hers, faint surprise as her pastry falls to ground, landing with a thud. He does not look back. She is too confused to chase. She looks up to see you, the witness, and you both grin in pain. This is how you found yourself standing in line with a stranger, relaying the events of the house party with rooftop vibes to her. While you talk your voice wobbles as you describe language plucked, plundered for the amusement of a few. She takes your elbow in her soft palm, asks if you're OK. You tell her that you're real cool because this is a place you have come to live. Come on then, she says, weaving between clustered joy, heading towards sound system where you feel bass slap thud, like a heartbeat. There is a pleasurable freedom in this slowness; where the frequencies lower and it is not so much a matter of the head but of the chest. She winds hips loose like elastic, takes your hand around her waist and encourages you to slow down. You take pleasure in the muddy fervour of a generous moment found under the miserly grey of a London sky on Carnival Monday. Unexpected miracle in these moments of freedom. Catch wines, sweat under arms and resting on foreheads, but no mind. Slow down and be guided by bass thudding in lazy rhythm. There's a nudge on your elbow, a young man offering small hazy fire between finger and thumb. Eyes crackle red with each soft gulp until pupils turn wide and Black. Slow down. Take pleasure. Your hand around her waist, small fire in palm, eyes ablaze. Loosen up, she says, and your hips break like the language. No need for mimicry. Miserly grey of a London sky on Carnival Monday, muggy heat stalling on bare back as you danced the day away with a stranger.

21

You are ending the summer like you began the winter together, twisting through the backroads, from New Cross to Deptford. You run into one of her friends, and you watch their conversation dance around each other, such easy rhythm, such beauty in being. Walking on, comfortably drunk. Sobriety extends a hand in the late-summer evening, and you both bat it away. Not now, not yet.

When you're a turn away from her flat, your fingers tangle. The seed you planted so long ago grown, the roots clutching in the darkness, pulling each other closer. Your lips meet under the canopy of a tree already showing autumnal symptoms.

You are ending summer, splitting a cigarette with her. She watches you fumble with the lighter. You're not a smoker, and she knows it, but the alcohol makes it easier to succumb to the idea. Besides, there's an intimacy to sharing this with her which you love. She takes the cigarette from you as she has done many times before, kindly, calmly, lighting up.

'You know,' she pauses to take a drag. 'OK, we're doing this now, I'm drunk, and we're doing this now.' Another drag. 'I was talking to my friends about you, about us. And there's parts of me you're gonna have to learn and understand.' She gazes at the ground for a moment. 'I haven't really done this before. I mean, I have, you know that. But this feels different.'

There are words and phrases rattling about your brain. You want to tell her, one day at a time, as you have been. You want to tell her you cannot wait to learn more about her, about all of her. But that you can and will wait, that time means nothing to you and her now, not really. You want to tell her how much you love her, but you're met with an impossibility, so instead you chuck under her chin and pull her towards you for a kiss, hoping she understands.

You are ending summer, hands resting on each other's thighs. Sitting across from each other on the train home, you were holding a gaze you could be forgiven for suggesting will never break. In moments such as these, time acts as it does in your relationship, falling away; past, present and future melding in the warmth of their touch. Neither of you wish to let this gaze go, but you know you must, if only briefly, knowing the return is an inevitability.

Later, lying in bed together, the feeling of timelessness heavier now you have come to a halt. This moment seems to be going on forever. What is it Kierkegaard says of the difference between a moment and an instant, of the fullness of time? Unimportant, as you fumble in the dark, knowing each other fully, in a way which will not be forgotten, in a way which feels right.

You are ending the summer, wondering how it is possible to miss someone before they have gone. There are lives moving around you but they are of little concern. Leaning against a noticeboard, your arms around her, running your chin over the softness of her shorn blonde head. You're both watching nervously for her train platform to be announced, and right on time –
    'That's you,' you say.
    'That's me,' she says.

She'll go from London to Holyhead and take the ferry to Dublin. On the platform, she kisses you, one foot on the train, one foot off. The whistle blows once. You need to step away from the train but you're not ready. You have never loved from a distance,

99

but then you have never known love like this. You want to tell yourself, and her, that it will be OK, that nothing will change, but you don't know. All too quickly, the whistle is blowing again, and the train doors are sliding shut. You hold off the tears until the train has pulled away, until you are stumbling down the platform. It is like the summer has been one long night and you have just woken up. It is like you both dived into the open water, but you have resurfaced with her elsewhere. It is like you formed a joint only to fracture, only to break. It is an ache you have not known and do not know how to name. It is terrifying. And yet, you knew what you were getting into. You know that to love is both to swim and to drown. You know to love is to be a whole, partial, a joint, a fracture, a heart, a bone. It is to bleed and heal. It is to be in the world, honest. It is to place someone next to your beating heart, in the absolute darkness of your inner, and trust they will hold you close. To love is to trust, to trust is to have faith. How else are you meant to love? You knew what you were getting into, but taking the Underground, returning home with no certainty of when you will see her next, it is terrifying.

*

'So now I have a place –'
    'Yes?'
'When can you come visit?'
'How soon is too soon?'
The next week, you're standing at her counter in Dublin cooking breakfast. The slithers of bacon sputter in the pan, while she taps on her laptop, planning things you can do together in the city.
    'We should definitely go to the Guinness Storehouse while you're here,' she says. 'There's something visually pleasing about watching it being made.'

'Let's do it. Guinness is Ghana's second national drink.'

'Really?' she says, raising an eyebrow.

'Yeah, it's like you go to a bar and instead of a pint of lager, you ask for a Guinness.'

'You're not just saying that to please me?'

'Promise.'

'OK, perfect.' She returns her gaze to her laptop. 'I mean, it's such a coupley thing to do, but whatever,' she says, unable to hide the glee this idea gives her. 'We'll do that tomorrow. I got a bunch of work to do today. And then tonight – we're going out.'

That first night: rum, cider, cider, interrupted by three stoners cleansing you both with sage, and a wonderful ensemble of improvised music. She asks you to describe her scent, and you are embarrassed, because you've thought about it before, and had an answer which slipped from your mouth: sweet, like flowers in fresh bloom. Not sickly but sweet enough to bring a smile to your face. That night you both get drunk and steal glasses from the bar. You tell her she deserves to be loved in the way you love her, and she starts to cry, quiet as rain.

The next morning, you gaze in the mirror with bloodshot eyes and ask if she has any paracetamol.

'I thought you didn't get hangovers,' she says.

'Oh, go away.'

You walk across Phoenix Park instead. The dredges of summer hang above you while she describes a summer before she knew you, spent working in Dublin. A time which imbued the city with a different feeling, one which allowed her to breathe here. It's a strange turn of phrase, you think, being allowed to breathe, having to seek permission for something so natural, the basis of life; in turn, having to seek permission to live. You're trying to remember the occasions when you couldn't breathe, when each inhale took effort, trying to bypass the weight lodged on the left side of your chest, trying to bypass the weight of having to know *how* you can breathe here –

'Where did you go?' Her eyes twinkle as they meet yours. You shake your head as the threads of thought come loose and fall away.

Walking towards the cinema, you pass a police van. They aren't questioning you or her but glance in your direction. With this act, they confirm what you already know: that your bodies are not your own. You're scared they will take them back, so you pull down the hood which is shielding you from the cold. She doesn't mention it – the unspoken exchange, the act of self-preservation – until you are sat outside her apartment block, watching a dog dance across the lawn with the moon as his spotlight.

'Are you all right?' She pauses as she lights her cigarette, taking a long drag. 'The police. Earlier. You good?'

'Yeah. Yeah, I'm good. Thinking about the film.'

The film you saw together that evening, Barry Jenkins' *If Beale Street Could Talk*, undid you. You didn't cry, just a twinge as something snapped into place, recognizing yourself in the actions of others. You didn't cry when Fonnie's cheekbones had gained shape and a purpose he didn't intend; when the tired man was on one side of the glass, and Tish on the other, equally wearied, cradling her unborn child, a protective forearm around her distended stomach. You didn't cry when Fonnie, stretched too far, snapped, trying to explain the intricacies of his current condition without the language to do so; Tish, collateral damage, a story you know too well. You didn't cry when she, unmoving, reached towards him to say, *I understand what you goin' through, I'm with you, baby.* No, you didn't cry, just a twinge as something snapped into place, recognizing yourself in the actions of others. The motivation of each character was the manifestation of love – she told you this – in their various actions. All actions are prayer, and these people have faith. Sometimes, this is all you can have. Sometimes, faith is enough.

That night, you dream the police wrote your death story and only included your name as a footnote. You jerk awake, squeezing her leg as you do; your limbs are wrapped together, and she lets out a small moan as you grapple for purchase. It's not the first time these anxieties have visited you in the night and, like before, the images remain long into your waking moments. You often worry that this will be your destiny, and, though she's always with you, she won't be there then – and you won't know who to call in that emergency. You wonder if the emergency has already begun. Evidence for this idea: the daily surprise of your enormous frame being walked into; being tailed by security guards in stores, both those who look like you and not; the scrubbing of identity with syllables that have never been your name. Further reading: jokes at your expense, implying a criminality or lack of intellect; others wanting to co-opt a word they dare not say in your presence, like they have not plucked enough from you; the wearying practice of being looked at, not seen.

You leave her in bed, and go first to the kitchen, for a glass of water, then to the living room. When the anxieties visit in the night, you like to watch rappers freestyling, because there is something wonderful about watching a Black man asked to express himself on the spot, and flourishing. You load up a video you've seen before on your phone and nod along in the dark. The first time you heard Kendrick say, *Ha-ha, joke's on you, high-five, I'm bulletproof, your shots'll never penetrate*, those lyrics sailed over your head, obscured by *that* instrumental and the playful jest of your favourite rapper. Now, you want to repurpose them for a future you could live in the present. You would like to be bulletproof. You would like to believe the shots will never penetrate. You would like to feel safe.

Over the next couple of days, you can't stop thinking about a scene in John Singleton's *Boyz n the Hood*, where Tre arrives at his girlfriend Brandi's house, after being stopped while driving by the police. The stop is routine. The policemen, one Black, one white, tell Tre and his friend to get out of the car. They bend them over the hood, while Tre, the more vocal of the pair, insists that they have done nothing wrong. With this insistence, Tre is asking the Black police officer searching him, *Why are you doing this?* This question sparks a wick forever smouldering. The policeman cocks his gun and digs it into Tre's neck. Tears stream down Tre's cheeks, meeting at his chin. The policeman doesn't answer directly, but with his actions he is saying, *I am doing this because I can.*

When Tre enters Brandi's living room, she asks him what's wrong. He replies, *Nothing.* He says this because to be him is to apologize and often that apology comes in the form of suppression, and that suppression is also indiscriminate. He explains that he is tired. He has had enough. That he wants to – There are not words for what he wants to do. He begins to swing at the air because he must get this out of him. He must explain. He must be heard. He swings at the air, large swipes, hoping to catch that which surrounds and often engulfs. He begins to moan, low and stifled. He wants to believe that Brandi's comforting will alleviate the situation, if only a little, but still the tears come. The mourning continues.

But we cool, we real cool, playing it cool. Keeping it real, cool, until –

'Are you OK?' she asks. 'Where did you go?'

'I'm good,' you say. And you are. Despite the fact the incident in Dublin a few days prior has stayed with you, despite the fact your concentration keeps drifting towards this memory and the paths it could have gone down, despite this, you're good in her presence. Or at least, you believe yourself to be.

'You don't have to be,' she says. She takes your hand in hers and rubs the thumb over the back of your palm. 'But share with me. I just want you to be OK.'

'Same. Same.' This is a different room from the one you know together, but the routine is the same. The dimness of a sidelight flooding the room in a short glow. Your smiling figures cast shadows against her yellow walls.

Your few days together have been spent doing nothing really, which is something, is an intimacy in itself. Outside now, the ground is wet, but it has not rained. You both prefer the warmth but you like the rain and its quiet noise. You spend your last day together trying to remain present. Akin to pushing Sisyphus' rock up one of the city's bigger hills, only for it to roll back down with every shove.

'You're far away,' she says, returning you to the present. 'Don't hide from me.'

Whenever she asks if you are OK, you nod, mute, convincing her, trying to convince yourself. Then she asks you, are you sure? To be you is to apologize and often that apology comes in the form of suppression and that suppression is indiscriminate. Except here you must unfold your arms and from your chest say, you are tired. That you have had enough. That you want to – There are not words for what you want to do. You begin to choke and gulp for air as tears stream down your cheeks. Moan, low and stifled. You must explain. You must be heard. You think you are alone in this until you realize, she is with you too. You want to believe that her comfort can alleviate the situation but only if you allow yourself to be held. You do not need to apologize here. When she asks, are you OK, do not fear the truth. Besides, she knows before you speak. There's no solace in the shade. Let yourself be heard and hear her words. Have faith. Suck at the snake's bite, spit out the venom at your feet. Gaze at the fading scar but do not dwell. Do not hide but do not dwell. There's no solace in the shade. Let yourself be heard and hear her words. Have faith.

Faith is turning off the light and trusting the other person will not murder you in your sleep. This is basic, audacious. Name your love. Name the sweet whispers exchanged in the darkness. Name the beauty of imagining your partner's fluttering eyelids as she dreams in her waking moments. How beautiful is beauty? You can find her lips with your eyes closed. *Nothing more durable than a feeling.* Tell her you're scared of being taken from her. Tell her what you struggle to tell yourself on some days. Tell her you love her and know what comes with these words. Describe the image of God in the darkness: the crooks of her long, slender limbs, catching light, even in the dark; features slack, eyes closed, lips turned up in a slight smile, cheeks pulling up with them, a small, pleasurable sigh slipping from her mouth every so often; the way her body tightens, loosens, tightens, loosens with every touch, every graze across the fine curve of her spine. Let her kiss the single tear. You don't know why you're crying. Sometimes, love aches. You're not sad but bowled over. Crumpled like a car crash. Tell her a story. Remind her about that time:

The fever dream of an evening, your minds swollen with heat. You and she swing your hips this way and that, letting rum dribble from the lips of cups onto the basement floor. A friend croons melancholy from the stage but the joy is not lost. Guitars strum sweet like the cocktails in your hands. You are more than the sum of your traumas, you decide, introducing her to your friends, your rhythms so fluid, a double act to be reckoned with. This is my friend, you say, words neither of you believe. (But can multiple truths not exist? Is anything definitive? Do you believe in permanence?) Anyway, this night is a fever dream and you allow yourselves to be led down a long stretch of road with the promise of another basement at the end of it. Is anything definitive? No, because you both change your minds when you reach the club. The fever has begun to rack your bodies and you shake with hunger. You split away from the group, because fever protects, as madness does. Chicken shop, sterile lighting, she hands over a plastic note, you give thanks, you curl hand around bare curve of hip, and she leans in, back, kiss on cheek, a shade of purple she carefully applied earlier. Midnight meal in hand, down a street on which you met another poet many years ago. Another basement. The poet leaned close and told you to loosen up during the warm-up act, so in no time you were in rhythm, fluid, an act to be reckoned with. Here, you sit on someone else's front steps, and you decide you believe in permanence. This definitive arrives when your best friend breaks the hot silence, cool and measured. She tells you she loves you and now you know that you don't have to be the sum of your traumas, that multiple truths exist, that you love her too.

Walt Dickerson wrote the piece 'To My Queen' for his wife. It's slow and contemplative, and reaches into extreme, beautiful depths to render a union in all its colour.

You don't have music, but you do have your way of seeing her. You do have a way of capturing her peaceful and energetic rhythm. You do have a way of portraying her joy.

You do have words.

23

To have a home is a luxury. To know someone before you knew them introduces a freedom previously unknown, when in their presence. Perhaps this is what home is: freedom. It's easy to stay furled up where you can't live, like folding a book in half on its spine to fit into pockets.

Sometimes you don't know why you feel this way. Heavy and tight and tired. It's like the incomplete version of yourself is in dialogue with the more complete parts. You had another conversation with your grandma, long after she passed. She came to you in a night vision and told you the body has memories. Told you to wear the scars on new skin. Let the woman you love kiss you and allow yourself to be called pretty. Unfurl, stretch out a spine made crooked by keeping small. There's only freedom here. You did not have a home coming into this world, but your world and your home have become synonymous with one another and they look something like this:

You run for the train. Someone left their umbrella under the seat in first class. It's raining. You crave blue skies and sunshine. She told you there was a hunger in your eyes, and you didn't disagree. You come from the same place. Same cloth. Gold woven into the kente. The shirt made for you from your grandmother's house is pale blue like the peace you crave. You want to give this to her. How do you say the things for which there is no language? Can you think of a time in which she was hungry too?

Returning from Dublin, on the train home, you don't know you're crying until the ugly splotches appear on the pages. Caught fast in your throat, syllables being rounded out and smoothed, language descending into noise. This is how you say those things for which there are no words. You want to scream. Two have become one but a hot blade has been taken to your skin and you have to wear these stories like scars. You want to wash them clean, and watch as she swims in the bath, slender limbs loose in the water. Love as a form of meditation; reaching towards a more honest expression of self. Remember that your body has memory. Scars do not always blemish. You kiss them and call her pretty. You're always surprised by the substance of her under your fingers. You want to lie beside her in the darkness and whisper your truths to her: *To my queen, forever is a mighty long time, but I knew you before I met you, so now we're free.* You didn't have a home coming into this world, but you're home now. You're home now.

24

'Are you getting a trim before I come home?'

'What's wrong with my hair?' you ask, running a hand over your scalp, feeling the tiny curls beginning to kink.

'Nothing's wrong per se,' she says. 'It would just be nice, you look handsome with a fresh trim.'

'You're digging yourself a hole here.'

You keep an eye for oncoming pedestrians as you walk, holding your phone slightly ahead of you, trying to keep your face in the frame of the video call. Four hundred miles away, she flops down on her bed, and reaches towards her camera with her finger, attempting to close the distance.

'Listen, I don't think it's a crime for me to want my man to look and feel good.'

'That's fair.'

'So are you gonna get one or not?'

'Maybe.'

'Maybe?'

You stop walking, right on time, and point the phone camera in front of you, to the barbershop.

'Ah,' she says. 'Great minds.' You sign off and go inside.

A haircut is an undertaking. You think of the waiting, waiting for your hairline to breach the line your barber had placed on your forehead a few weeks before. You think of the decision to go, a gamble in itself; your barber, like most barbers, doesn't have a schedule. Today, as you enter – you're early, early is always better – there's a child in the seat, bawling as the barber takes a metal-toothed comb to hair which has curled and twisted, roots and undergrowth merged together to form a dense, kinky bush on his head. His mother watches on as the barber attempts to tease the comb through hair which won't reciprocate the effort. Leon, your barber, doesn't give up. He oils the hair with his own hands, so it is a smooth journey for the comb, rather than the scratches like twigs snapping. He takes care, and the child calms, comforted by the endeavour and the barber's instructions for kink prevention.

It's not long before the barber gives a nod in your direction to say it's your turn. You sit in the chair, letting him drape the apron over you which he cinches at the neck. He takes a set of clippers in hand; the buzz of the machine operates at a vibration that speaks to you and encourages you to do the same.

'Wha' ya want?' he asks.

'Skin fade,' you say. 'Keep the top, please.'

'The beard?'

'You can shave it off.'

The barber works quietly, murmuring to himself. You close your eyes and allow yourself to drift away. You're safe here. You are able to say what you want and know it is OK. You know there is a semblance of control here that you don't often have. You know you can be free here. Where else can you guarantee Black people gather? This is ritual, shrine, ecstatic recital. With every visit, you are declaring that you love yourself. You love yourself enough to take care. And it's here, in the barbershop, that you can be loud and wrong and right and quiet. It's here you can lean across to the next man, and state your case, ask for clarification, enquire into that which you don't know. It is here you can laugh, it is here you can be serious. It is here you can breathe. It is here you can be free. Especially with your barber. What you say to him, stays.

'How you been?' he asks.

'Can't complain, can't complain. You?'

'Just came back from holiday. I was in Ghana.'

'How was it?'

'My body is back but my mind is still there.'

'It's a special place.'

'You've been?'

'A while ago. That's where my family is from.'

'That makes sense. You've got that energy, that rhythm. Everyone is so calm there. They take their time. They eat, they drink, they laugh. They live well. And I tell you something else,' he says, tapping your shoulder. 'You don't have to worry about looking like us when you're out there.'

'I hear that,' you say.

'That kinda freedom?' He shakes his head and continues to work the clippers over your scalp.

'It's just different,' he starts up a few moments later. 'The sunshine. The climate, it makes me want to do things. To be out in the world. When I'm here, winter comes, and I hibernate.' You both laugh. 'I wasn't meant to be here, you know? I've been in this country years and years, before you were born. Came here, had my children, my children are having children. And still, it doesn't feel like home. Doesn't feel like I'm wanted here. Hmm. What is it you do? For work?'

'I'm a photographer.'

'See, you don't have to be here. You have another half?'

You pull your phone from your pocket and flash the photo of her on your home screen.

'She's beautiful. Want my advice? Find a place you can call home. This isn't it. It's hard to just be in this place. So much goes on that you don't even realize until you realize, you know what I mean? Go somewhere you can be free. Where you don't have to think too tough about what you do before you do it. Find a place you can call home.' He taps your shoulder once more. 'You're all done, young man.'

Outside, you stand and brush the tiny flecks of dark hair from the back of your neck. A light breeze grazes your freshly shorn head. You begin to untangle your headphones for your walk home, and your barber joins you on the stoop of his shop. He hums, watching traffic pass on this main road. From his pocket, he pulls a bag of tobacco, some rolling papers. He opens the tiny bag, and there's the smell of something sweeter, something darker, heavy like musk but light as a cloud. You watch as he pinches the tip of a paper and, tucking the bag between his stomach and arm, lines the joint with a healthy serving. He rolls it back and forth, and lifts it to his mouth to seal, humming all the while. The song is a loop, a light number which dances up and down the scales. This is a ritual, you think, as he twists the end and pulls out a lighter. The joint sparks alight on the first try and your barber pulls smoke into his lungs.

He nudges you, arm outstretched, the joint an offering at the shrine. You take it from him and inhale as deep as it will go. You feel your brain go hazy and dark immediately.

'Careful now,' he says. 'Not too quick. This one is strong. It'll help you forget.'

He opens his mouth as you take another pull, and he begins to sing. The tune is so sweet, like that of a bird who has learned to fly in his gilded cage. The flame smoulders in your hands and he passes you the lighter. Another pull. Deeper, darker. All the while, he sings. His features slack, the noise deliberate. He moves his shoulders in a slow rhythm, and you do the same, rocking side to side, as his voice gains volume, as the fire smoulders in your hand, as you stand outside of the shrine, as you complete this ritual, soundtracked by his ecstatic recital.

The next toke takes you from joy towards a darkness. You begin to panic, and listen for the barber's song, but it only leads you deeper, darker. It's an easy route. You are in sudden pain. You thought you had sealed off this path today but you are being confronted with your ache. You stroke each of the dogs' heads and watch them cower at your gall. You're descending at a hellish pace but there's no fire here, the fire brought you here. In this nightmare, there is only water lapping at your feet, nipping at your heels. Show me your scars, the monster asks. Show me where the snake wrapped itself around your arm and sunk its teeth into soft flesh. You roll up your sleeves and show him the holes littering your limbs. Come out of the shadows, he says. There's no solace in the shade. Show me where it hurt, he says. Don't wait for the water to rise. The water won't save you. You look down and see a warbled reflection in the ripple of the black depths. God has many faces. Many voices. A song in the darkness. Have faith. Suck at the snake's bite, spit out the venom at your feet. To swallow is to suppress. To be you is to apologize and often that apology comes in the form of suppression, and that suppression is indiscriminate. Spit it out. Don't wait for the water to rise. Don't apologize. Forgive yourself.

'Careful now,' you hear again, and you're dragged from the reverie. The flame smoulders in your hand. Your barber is still singing, sweet as a songbird.

'What are you trying to forget?' you ask him.

He takes the joint from you, pulling smoke into his own lungs. He steps out from the shade of the building into a shaft of sunlight.

'I don't know. It's a feeling. It's something *deep*. It's something in me.' He laughs a little to himself. 'It doesn't have a name, but I know what it feels like. It hurts. Sometimes, it hurts to be me. Sometimes, it hurts to be us. You know?'

You understand. Often, you're not given a name. You would like to take the liberty. But even if you don't name yourself or name your experience, it remains. Rising to the surface, oil swimming in water. You want to lay claim to this life you lead. Here, standing next to this man, the sun slipping through his glasses, splitting the light in his clear brown eyes into yellow, red, hazel, green, you aren't scared to say you are scared and heavy. You hope he is encouraged to do the same. You get the feeling he feels how you do sometimes: like you're bobbing and weaving in the ocean and it's a fight you didn't sign up for. You don't want to go under. You can swim in water, but the oil will kill you. You don't want to die. This is basic and audacious, but you want to lay claim to it while you still can.

You prod the pain in your left side and want to be made light. You pray with every action this will not be the day. Every day is the day, but you pray this day is not the day. Your mother prays every day that this will not be the day. You hear her through the bathroom door, praying for her sons, even as you play rapper while you swim in shallow water. No one has bars harder than your mum as she prays for you every day that this will not be the day. You know that this day could be the day but still you laugh it off when your partner says she's concerned for you to travel at night. You flash the smile of a king but you both know regicide is rife. You wash off dark soapsuds in the shower and pray that today is not the day. If you give a name to this day does that mean this life is yours? To name: basic, audacious. Lay claim, take power, take aim, this is yours. This act is like bringing a butter knife to a gunfight. You want to play rapper so you can say, *I know that line went over your heads*. You want to lie in darkness beside your partner and talk death like you have nothing to fear. You do not want to die before you can live. This is basic and audacious, but you want to lay claim to it while you still can.

Leon, the barber, beautiful man, wise as an oak, dreads flapping with excitement, stubs out the joint and announces he has a present for you. You follow him back into the barbershop. He heads to a bookshelf in the corner, the shelves themselves bending in the middle under the weight of the stacks. You don't remember seeing other people enter the shop, but four men wait patiently on the long sofa pushed against the wall. Leon riffles quickly, knowing where each book is, and pulls one out, handing it to you. You read the cover: *The Destruction of Black Civilization* by Chancellor Williams.

'Thank you,' you say. 'I'll bring it back next time I get a cut.'

'Nah, man, that's all you. That one, that's a book I return to a few times a year. It's my favourite gift to give. I have plenty copies. Keep it, lemme know what you think.'

You smile, and as you go to dap him, the enormous glass window of the shopfront shatters, glass raining to the ground. The chaos is immediate. Every man is on his feet. You take stock: a figure, black T-shirt, scrambling across the floor. You recognize this man, you've seen him bopping around ends; no, you *know* this man, you have shared space and time with him. But there's no time to tell this story. Right now, you're concerned with what lies on the other side of the shopfront: five men demanding access to the young man who fell through the glass. They're shouting and pointing and the glint of light from something in one of their hands clenches your body, twists your spirit. You can hear Leon telling everybody to calm down. You can hear the young man panting. You can hear the men in the shop shouting too, protective. You can hear fear. You can hear sirens in the distance. You can hear panic. Those outside the shop are unrelenting, but refuse to cross the threshold of this shrine, the barbershop. I don't know you, man, you've got the wrong guy, you hear the young man say. His name comes to you: Daniel. You can hear Daniel's fear. The sirens grow closer. All those present grow more fearful in the presence of the siren because when they, the police, are close, you lose your names and you have all done wrong. Those outside the shop are unrelenting, they want Daniel, they are shouting at him to come out, come out before they come in. But the sirens are growing closer, and they want their liberty more than they want Daniel. Three of them start to shift. One remains with the glint in his hand. It must be his grievance. The others insist it's not worth it and tug at him to come, let's go, let's go, they say. He gives in, his face contorted, unrelenting. This is the face of a man who will try again another day. They scramble and scarper. The room takes a collective breath as you wait for the police to arrive.

When they do, the chaos is immediate. They're shouting and pointing and the glint of dark light from guns in all of their hands clenches your body, twists your spirit. You can hear Leon telling everybody to calm down. You can hear Daniel panting. You can hear the men in the shop shouting too, protective. You can hear fear. You can hear bodies being crumpled. A knee on a crooked back, a book folded in on its spine. We haven't done anything, we haven't done anything, you hear Daniel say. They do not listen. You are heavy and scared. They pat you down and riffle through pockets and ask what it is you're hiding. You want to say the ache, but you don't think they'd understand. Not when they are complicit. This goes on until they grow tired, they grow bored, they lose focus, there is a call somewhere else. Just doing our jobs, they say. You're free to go now, they say.

'Are we ever?' Leon asks.

There's an anger you have. It is cool and blue and unshifting. You wish it was red so it would explode from your very being, explode and be done with, but you are too used to cooling this anger, so it remains. And what are you supposed to do with this anger? What are you supposed to do with this feeling? Some of you like to forget. Most of you live daily in a state of delusion because how else is one meant to live? In fear? Some days, this anger creates an ache so bad you struggle to move. Some days, the anger makes you feel ugly and undeserving of love and deserving of all that comes to you. You know the image is false, but it's all you can see of yourself, this ugliness, and so you hide your whole self away because you haven't worked out how to emerge from your own anger, how to dip into your own peace. You hide your whole self away because sometimes you forget you haven't done anything wrong. Sometimes you forget there's nothing in your pockets. Sometimes you forget that to be you is to be unseen and unheard, or it is to be seen and heard in ways you did not ask for. Sometimes you forget to be you is to be a Black body, and not much else.

A few hours later, you're walking up the road to grab a patty from the Caribbean takeaway. You're hungry for the sweet yellow pastry, filled with spicy meat. You're hungry for comfort. So you're walking, a route you take every day, along the main road of Bellingham, when you see Daniel, cycling towards you. He dismounts as he reaches the Morley's, and he daps you with a wide smile on his face, his hips moving in time to whatever spills from his headphones. It is like all has been forgotten. It is like you can let go of that anger for a moment. His pleasant rhythm is infectious and you two step around each other, before laughing and splitting away, he heading into the chicken shop, you a few doors down. Inside the Caribbean takeaway, a dub bassline rocks the windows. You spy the cook tying up his dreads in the kitchen before emerging into the main area, crooning, 'I'm still in love with you,' interpolating the classic. It makes you think of her, of playing this song, holding her neat waist, pulling her close, closer, feeling her smile as she lets the back of her neck settle into your chest.

'What can I get for you, brother?' he asks. You decide, on impulse, to treat yourself to a serving of mac and cheese. You watch as he packs some wings into a box as an extra, and when you try to pay for them, he shakes his head.

'I can tell you need some good food,' he says. You pound fists, and depart.

As you emerge, you are greeted with a sound the colour of James Brown's scream, pale and broken. Something has seized the body of the person the scream came from. The sound lasts seconds but only grows stronger. And then, for a moment, there is silence. There's commotion, panicked movement, a car speeding away, a bike laid on its side, the owner laid out on the ground.

You're running towards him. There's surprise on his face because he allowed himself to forget about today. And who can blame him? You reach for his hand and ask if he needs anything. He doesn't dap your hand this time, because all his strength left him with that scream. He doesn't laugh or smile or cry. We need an ambulance, someone says. There's a lot of blood, you need to hurry. The young man on the ground shakes his head. You didn't realize you were still holding his hand but you let go now. His rhythm is infectious and you are stood stock-still. You have known him by many names, but today he was Daniel.

25

'What's your trim saying?'

You're sitting amongst your own mess, holding the phone to your ear. When you came home, you trashed your room with the furious ease of a tornado. It was juvenile, and good to feel in control of something, but now she has called and the dust has settled and you have run out of things to say.

'Hey – you there?' she asks.

'Yeah.'

'I didn't hear from you. I was a little worried but I thought you might've got caught up in work or something.'

'Something like that. Sorry.'

'Don't be silly. How was your day?'

'OK,' you say.

A pause. 'Are you all right?'

You begin to sob, gasping for air. You're suffocating in your own room. You hang up the phone. You are hiding your whole self away because you haven't worked out how to emerge from your own anger, how to dip into your own peace.

She calls right back.

'What's going on?'

'Nothing.'

'Nothing? You don't sound OK. That sound you just made . . . just talk to me, please.'

'There's nothing.'

'It doesn't sound like nothing.'

'There's nothing.'

'You're not being fair. I'm really here just trying to check you're OK because I care and all I'm getting is *nothing, nothing, nothing*.'

'I don't know what to say to you.'

'It feels like you're pushing me away. Like there's something wrong and you just won't tell me. It's felt like this for a while.'

'There's nothing.'

'You're not being honest with me. I can't do this if you won't be honest with me.'

'There's nothing. Can't you just drop it?'

'Fine. Whatever.'

On the line, static; the dam has burst, and anything else said will be drowned by the sound of rushing water. And like that, a joint, fractured, broken.

The line goes dead and the ocean has stilled.

You stop calling. You stop returning her calls. A few days later, you turn off your phone entirely. You've been keeping her at arm's length since she moved to Dublin, and now, you push, knowing she can't just make the short journey across south-east London. You push, knowing it's easier to retreat than showing her something raw and vulnerable. Than showing her you. You live in a haze, cool and blue, light with anger, heavy with melancholy. You live at a pace in which you are unmoving. You live as a version less than yourself. You sob often, suffocating wherever you go. You are hiding yourself. You are running, stuck in place. You are scared and heavy.

You ache. You ache all over. You are aching to be you, but you're scared of what it means to do so.

You're sitting at your desk, letting the time pass until you can sleep and have a brief reprieve. You've since cleaned the mess you made, but your mind is chaotic.

You're reading but taking little in. You're looking at images but not seeing. You're listening to music but the melodies are dull, the drums lack punch, the lyrics come towards you and join the wash of your own thoughts, like a tide coming and going, coming and going, the tow tugging you this way and that, and all you can do is stay still. You don't have it in you to move any more. You don't have it in you to swim.

It's harmful where you're going. You know this, and still you go, you hide. It's easier this way. You don't want to have to question why Daniel shook his head when someone was calling an ambulance for him. You don't want to admit that he too knew he had been marked for destruction, that he had spent a life so close to death that it was less a life lived and more one survived. When the time came, he was ready to rest. You aren't ready to confront these facts and what it might mean for you. You are scared and you are heavy, and you are not ready.

A knock at your door. Your brother comes in without waiting for an answer. He's been checking in once a day since you lost your friend. Your curtains are drawn so you couldn't tell what the time is, but as he enters, sunlight flickers. He leaves the door open and the light streams in. You recognize the shadows on your walls: leaves swaying in the breeze at golden hour, the shapes soft, the movement easy, entrancing.

'Yo,' he says.

'Yo.'

'You spoken to her?'

'Nah.'

Your brother sits on the edge of your bed.

'Are you gonna speak to her?'

You turn to him now.

'What would I even say?'

He shrugs. 'Something. Anything. Tell her how you are, she'll wanna hear from you.'

'I know.' You know this, and still you hide.

'Man,' he says. 'How are you feeling?'

You open your mouth to speak, and your body begins to shake and wobble. You open your mouth to speak, but you don't have the words. Your brother knows what it is like to not have the words, and he can see the panic rising in your body, he can see you're about to start gulping for air, he sees there are tears on the way, so he holds you, he holds you close, he holds you with care. You allow yourself to be held, as you have done for him before. You allow yourself to be soft and childlike in his arms. You allow yourself to break.

You're coming out of your house, a week after you've turned your phone off, when something small and hard and purposeful shoves you in the back, connecting with bone and tissue and muscle. You're sent barrelling forwards into the road.

'What the fuck?'

A flurry of long limbs comes towards you, and you push them away, separating from the owner, gaining perspective.

She's standing in front of you, breathing heavy.

'What are you doing here?' you ask.

'What is your problem?'

'Pardon?'

'Why is it that if I want to speak to my boyfriend, I have to come all the way from Dublin to see you?'

You don't have words.

'I tried texting, calling, I asked your friends, I asked everyone! Do you know how worried I've been? You're so selfish. So, so selfish. You're not thinking of us, you're just thinking of you when you do this. And this isn't the first time. Since I've been back at uni, whenever you feel like it, you've just gone –' She mimes being pushed away.

'I didn't ask much of you. I just wanted you to be honest. I wanted you to *communicate*. Just open your mouth and talk to me. But instead you shut me out. You've literally locked yourself away from me. Can you imagine how that feels? Can you? Put yourself in my shoes. Stand where I'm standing. Do it!' She takes a step back, and manoeuvres you to where she stood, so that you are facing an empty space. 'How does that feel? Hmm?'

'Not good.'

'Of course it doesn't feel good! *Fuck!*'

'Hey –'

'No, no, no. You're gonna listen to me. You're moving mad. Do you know how much we risked getting into this? Do you know how guilty I felt for so long? I was still with Samuel when I met you and a few months later, we're the best of friends, and a few months after that, we're partners. Do you know how long that's been for me? Do you know how many people in my circle have shut me out because of what they *think* happened? But did I care? No. Because when I met you, I thought, I love this man. We've always been able to talk to each other. About anything and everything. I didn't have to be anything but myself around you. I thought we could be honest with each other. I thought we could be honest here.'

It's easier to hide in your own darkness, than to emerge, naked and vulnerable, blinking in your own light. Even here, in plain sight, you're hiding. She's right about all she has said. Here was a place you could be honest. This was a place you could be yourself. This was a place where you didn't have to explain, but now she's standing in front of you and she's asking you to explain. You wish you had the words, no, you wish you had the courage to climb up from whatever pit you have fallen into, but right now, you do not. You watch her watching your internal struggle. Her features soften. She reaches for you and you step back. You feel dirty with your heaviness and fear and you don't want to stain her. She too steps back, your backwards movement like a shove in her chest. There is a difference between being looked at and being seen. She sees you now, she sees what is being presented to her. She shakes her head, and begins to pull the hoody she is wearing off her body. It's yours, or at least it was. You gave it to her but now she dashes it in your direction. She walks away from you. You do not chase her. You stand there, frozen, hiding in plain sight.

26

You have been booked for a portrait session and you're on the way to a studio, because you must go on. This is your life now. This is what you have chosen. So you're on the way to the studio and it's a day where the sky is giving away nothing, stuck between bleary autumn and an empty winter. You're listening to Earl Sweatshirt's 'Grief' because that song aches but it ends with a joyful refrain. You're trying to feel something, anything, but you are numb. The music you had with her has stopped. You're trying to play the same song you played together but two has become one. You and she were forever improvising, but two has become one, and without her there's nowhere for you to twist and turn. The music has stopped.

If the heart always aches in the distance between the last time and the next, then heartbreak comes in the unknown, the limbo, the infinity.

You've been booked for a portrait session and you're in the studio. You've asked the person you're shooting to relax a little. His shoulders are bunched up, the tension in his jaw causing his eyes to narrow. He doesn't know what to do with his hands and holds them, holding himself, folded inwards. Relax, you say. He tries to smile, but cannot. He's trying to put himself at ease, but he cannot. You realize you are gazing in a mirror. The artist always gives something to the portrait, and here you're seeing what manifests when you cannot say what you feel: it escapes anyway. You excuse yourself to the bathroom. You stand alone. You gaze in the mirror and you see that you are not a coward but you have done a cowardly thing and that you're not malicious but you have hurt her and you're not an embarrassment but you are ashamed. The music has stopped. The rest is noise. You cry. You cry through your own shame and ache and pain. You hold yourself. You wrap your long arms around your own body and allow yourself to be soft and childlike in your own arms.

You allow yourself to break.

27

It's quieter, here, on the other side of freedom. You could be elsewhere. You walk beside the dog, entering a gated community, the door swinging shut behind you. The soft gloom falls off your shoulders in the warm evening. Earlier, the dog had nudged your stomach, clambering beside you on the corner of the sofa you were curled up in. You held on tight while your mind spiralled in its noisy confines. But it's quieter here. There's no one but you and the dog. You watch it bound across pedestrianized streets, writing its own story. You decide freedom might be a narrative. Freedom might be in the place beyond the fence. Freedom might be inviting others over the boundary. You take photos of the dog pounding around and think of sending them to her, but it's far too late for that. It occurs to you this freedom might be temporary but you're here, in this world.

It's been a long time since you wore your hoody on roads. It snowed heavily for a week in the past winter. Every day, you would finger the threaded cotton of your black hoody, until the smell of her began to disappear. Your life with her unstitched in the same way, becoming more undone with each passing day. You stood to the side and watched your relationship fall apart. It was easier to do this. It was simpler and cowardly. To love someone like that, to know how beautiful and wholesome and healing such a love is, and to turn your back on it required no strength at all. You have always wondered under what conditions unconditional love breaks, and you believe that betrayal might be one of them.

★

Six months have passed since the day she confronted you. Six months have passed since the day she said she could see you and asked you to see her too. Six months have passed since you were unable to offer your own vulnerability; she made the decision to walk away and you did not chase. Today, you have decided to pull on your hoody, for comfort, and speak your truth. You do not want to hide any more, even if it hurts.

This morning is the first in a long time you have woken with a funk in your step. James Brown would've been proud. You are sure you all have the scream in your chests, waiting to emerge. You are sure these screams don't have to be pale and bloody but full and vital.

Speaking of James Brown's scream, you want to riff, and talk about a Friday evening, long ago, before the fracture and the break. Uncle Wray and his Nephew making an appearance. Asking the smart speaker to play rapper Playboi Carti. It's said he's mumbling but you hear something else. He too is filling the pocket, darting in the space between the 808 and the glittering melody, closing the distance with his short lines and ad libs. Just as on that first night, when two strangers closed a distance, held close by melody. Anyway, regarding Carti – less heady, more from the chest; less thought, more honest, more intention. They say he's mumbling but you hear something else. It makes you move.

You came here, really, to whisper in the dark, like when you used to turn the lights out, and you were twisted in her covers, seeing nothing but her familiar shape.

You want to tell her of your parents. Your father on a Saturday afternoon bent over the sound system, scrolling until he retrieves the memory captured in song. Sweet croon, daytime lullaby. The words we have for this feeling are not enough but perhaps the melody? Perhaps the bass, slapping, thudding. A heartbeat. Perhaps your parents grooving in their own living room, slow croon. Your mother asks if and where they play slow jams in the city. You promise to find a place as they two-step in unison.

You want to ask her if she remembers what song was playing when you were on the train home. You had been dancing all evening in a basement full of jazz musicians, both dancers and performers improvising, separate and apart. When you boarded the train, a handful of these musicians sat in the adjacent seats. You began to gush to each other. Someone referred to the night as a spiritual experience. The frequencies were right. There, gathered together, the energy spilled over. One of them began to sing. The percussionist procured a shaker and kept you all in time as you all moved, alone in this train carriage, together, improvising, dancing in protest, moving in joy.

You want to ask her if she remembers such freedom.

You want to tell her of the young man you saw, opposite on the Overground. Shoes the colour of a clear sky, tattoo clasping his bicep. He drinking from a black can, you from a glass bottle. Headphones atop both your heads. He caught your eye. You nodded to each other and raised your drinks in joyous greeting. The gaze required no words at all, no, it was an honest meeting. You want to tell her that, in this *instant*, one which was filled with the fullness of time, you loved this man. Loved him like kin. You had no intentions of making a home in each other, but only to stay for a moment, only to feel safe for a moment.

You want to tell her there are some things you won't heal from, and there is no shame in your hurt. You want to tell her that in trying to be honest here, you dug until shovel met bone, and you kept going. You want to tell her it hurt. You want to tell her that you have stopped trying to forget that feeling, that anger, that ugly, and instead have accepted it as part of you, along with your joy, your beauty, your light. Multiple truths do exist, and you do not have to be the sum of your traumas.

You came here, to the page, to ask for forgiveness. You came here to tell her you are sorry that you wouldn't let her hold you in this open water. You came here to tell her how selfish it was to let yourself drown.

You came here to tell the truth. That you are scared and heavy. That sometimes this weight is too heavy. The ache in your chest fills, bulbous and stretched, and though you wish it would, the ache will not burst.

Saidiya Hartman describes the journey of Black people from chattel to men and women, and how this new status was a type of freedom if only by name; that the re-subordination of those emancipated was only natural considering the power structures in which this freedom was and continues to operate within. Rendering the Black body as a species body, encouraging a Blackness which is defined as *abject, threatening, servile, dangerous, dependent, irrational and infectious,* finding yourself being constrained in a way you did not ask for, in a way which could not possibly contain all that you are, all that you could be, could want to be. That is what you are being framed as, a container, a vessel, a body, you have been made a body, all those years ago, before your lifetime, before anyone else who is currently in your lifetime, and now you are here, a body, you have been made a body, and sometimes this is hard, because you know you are so much more. Sometimes this weight is too heavy. The ache in your chest fills, bulbous and stretched, and though you wish it would, the ache will not burst. You are thinking of booking into therapy, and explaining that you feel like you were made a body, a vessel, a container, and that you are worried, because the days when you believe this are becoming more frequent.

You came here to say you are scared you have long been marked for destruction.

You came here to talk about the seagull. Does she remember? There was no blood. Sprawled out on its back, wings splayed. Head at a peculiar angle, a part of itself forced into where it couldn't fit. The theories came with each observation. From a height, perhaps? A brave bird perched on a balcony, given a nudge. But would it not fly? Would there not be more of a mess, rather than the majestic way this creature had been laid to rest? There was no blood. You concluded the seagull had its neck snapped by human hand and you wanted to know how, who and why. You went back and forth but grew no closer to a complete truth. You could only guess. The spectacle occupied your lives for a few more moments. You watched the cars avoid the dead; you imagined the drivers nudging the steering wheel slightly, before readjusting their course and driving on.

Teju Cole describes how death arrives absurdly, in the midst of banality. In his essay 'Death in the Browser Tab', he talks about Walter Scott. This man, Walter Scott, knows that while he is being questioned by a police officer, a rigid tension exists that, when shattered, will result in his destruction. Cole is talking about watching a man who knows he is dying, who has been playing it cool, playing it cool, until the moment he flees, for freedom, because freedom is really the distance between hunter and prey. Cole talks about being stunned. *Plunged into someone else's crisis, someone else's horror.* But doesn't he know? Of course he does. But what do you do with the things you don't want to know?

You came here to talk about one of your earliest memories, in which you did not have the luxury of a browser tab. It was a window first, an open window. A stillness to the soft shine of spring. Quiet, here. Your father parked on the wrong side of the petrol pump, but you were in the midst of a fuel shortage so watched as he dragged the hose round the pale green of the family car. You leaned your head out of the open window to smile at him. He was not there. His body was stood to attention, caught in the rigid tension of a man who knows that, if this shatters, it will result in his destruction. The police officer saw your father watching a young man being questioned and your father turned away, placing imagined distance between hunter and prey. Your father rushed towards the pay kiosk and you imagine he was flustered, forgoing his usual charm, dull glitter in his eye like a speck of dust. All the while, the young man was being questioned by two policemen. He was beautiful. A child, somebody's child! Don't you lie to me, you hear one say to him. You didn't have a name for it then, the shoulders hitched up to his ears, eyes widened, the stuttered profession of innocence. You looked to your mother for explanation or clarity, because there didn't appear to be reason for this. You wanted to know how, who and why. Turning back to the window, a flash of light like a quick shadow. The young man's hair had escaped his hairband. He was trying to fly away, towards a freedom he knew could only be found in the distance between hunter and prey. A nudge and he was sprawled out on his back, wings splayed. Head at a peculiar angle, a part of himself forced into where he couldn't fit. Arms, too, twisted behind his back as blows rained from black batons painting beautiful skin with fresh wounds. Flashes of darkness, where the light was leaving him. There was no blood. Death is not always physical.

You came here to say there was no blood when, a couple of years ago, your discomfort emerged into a fresh pain. You were coming down a set of marble stairs, running a hand along a smooth banister, when it struck like dull lightning to the back. By the time you were at the foot of the stairs, you were folded over. A book creased on its spine. They sat you down and asked where it hurt. You couldn't discern at first, but homed in on a difficulty whenever you inhaled, exhaled. Left side. This was now an emergency. There was no blood but you were thinking of apoptosis, a process by which the body engineers its own demise by programming the cells to warp and morph towards their eventual death. The body kills itself, slowly. There is no blood. There was no blood.

The paramedic arrived in minutes, like he had been waiting for an emergency. He asked, do you know what is happening to you? No diagnosed conditions, no. He checked your blood pressure and commented on your slow, lumbering heart rate.

Athlete?

Former, you said. Used to play a lot of basketball.

Hmm, he said. And in the gap between what he has said and what he has not, you're thinking about cell death, how the body kills itself from the inside out, how hurt can manifest in various forms.

Let's do an ECG, to be safe.

You watched the machine write your story in regular rhythm, the jagged loop constant. The paramedic pointed to a short jut in each of these, and said you had an arrythmia. He said it was hard to tell if this was something you've had forever or something you have developed in the past year, or something which had come on that day. You're not one to worry, or to have others worry for you, and besides the pain had subsided, so it was probably nothing, right? It's probably nothing, the paramedic confirmed. He recommended painkillers and rest and to take it easy.

The thing lingered, dormant. When it emerged once more, you were in the British Library, listening to a group of readings. Later, at dinner, you shivered with a warm drink in hand and smiled through the discomfort. It was only when you returned home and collapsed onto your sofa that you began to think of cell death once more and how hurt might change how this process occurs.

That year, you had been aching. You lost yourself. You lost your grandma. They killed Rashan and Edson, from the outside in. And like an echo, they pushed you up against the wall and you scraped your hands trying to find somewhere to hold on. Your breath was short, even without their fingers curling on your neck. Things were falling apart from the root. Irregular rhythm. It's probably nothing. And yet. Take it easy.

You heed the advice and turned off the lights. You turned on a film and cried in the dark.

You cry in darkness. Death is not always physical, and crying is not always an expression of pain. You've said a lot, but you came to speak of the stillness of an autumnal evening, trees boughed towards you in the dark of dusk. You held her at arm's length. You told her not to look at you because when your gazes meet you cannot help but be honest. But remember Baldwin's words? *I just want to be an honest man and a good writer.* Hmm. Honest man. You're being honest, here, now.

You came here to speak of what it means to love your best friend. A direct gaze. An honest man. You're searching for words, but none will do. Ask: if flexing is being able to say the most in the least amount of words, is there a greater flex than love? The gaze requires no words at all; it is an honest meeting.

You came here to ask if she will look at you, while you tell her this story.

This is not an overstatement. You are dying. You young boys are dying. You kill your mothers in the process. The grief makes them tired. The effort makes them tired. This living is precarious. Imagine leaving your house and not knowing if you will return intact. You do not need to imagine. You live precarious. You cool, you real cool, playing it cool. Keeping it real, cool, until – Sigh into the darkness. Daily strain makes chest tight. You have been torn and furled, like they ripped the pages out of your book and crumpled them like wastepaper. This is how you die. This is how young boys die. This is how your mothers and partners and sisters and daughters die too. The grief makes them tired. The effort makes them tired. This living is precarious and could make light work of your life at any time. Imagine knowing that your wholeness could be split at any moment, so you live in pieces. You live broken, you live small, lest someone makes you smaller, lest someone break you. You are Black body, container, vessel, property. You are treated as such because property is easy to destroy and plunder. You do not need to imagine a life you already lead. It is precarious to sigh into darkness and say you are real cool because that poem ends with you dying soon. You have been torn and furled and you're scared you will flutter away in a small breeze. Forever unseen. This is how young boys die. This is how your mothers and partners and sisters and daughters die too. The grief makes you tired. The effort makes you tired.

You're longing for the moment you saw four Black boys in a Beemer. At the traffic lights, they shaved off the hood. Sweet

Mary drifted towards your nostrils. They bucked their heads in rhythm like a bobbing buoy. It's joy, the feeling that bounced about your chest, that these young men could be driving, yellow beams spilling from street lights onto their faces, the light in their eyes the brightest, a life uninhibited, even if it is only brief, it is theirs, this space, in a moving vehicle, an 808 kicking at the body of the car, a childish guffaw, jokes only for them. Towards the end of the laughter, as it trailed away into the night, as their tyres screeched, engine revving, the joy morphed, returning to its usual form. Joy is not always entirely pleasurable, so it was a bonus when it sidled alongside the usual terror, the tumbling tumult that touches you in such instances.

This nostalgia is sickly sweet, and it hurts. You're thinking of springtime, sunshine, clouds clear and the colour of the sky is sweet like a baby's warbled delight for their mother. You hold your mother tight when you say goodbye to her. Hear her wheeze from a chest made tight from years of work. Never the same after the year it snowed, '93. Trudging through white ash to stack shelves. Even the protests from her best friend could not prevent her manager from taking sour revenge on her refusal of his advances. He ordered her to work in the freezer until her teeth chattered and she could not feel her fingertips on her own bulbous stomach, heavy with life brewing. You owe a lot to your mother and one day, you will tell that story, but for now, you're thinking of springtime, sunshine, clouds clear. You hold your mother tight: soft musk, light wheeze, still life. As you walk through the front gate blossom showers, like burst bag of glitter. Overhead. They're shaving trees bare, indecently exposed against the backdrop of springtime, sunshine. You wave at the old woman who waves back at you every morning, seated against the window of her sheltered accommodation. She gives you a thumbs-up. You wonder what, if anything, she is waiting for. Anyway, there's nothing unusual as you select Dilla – *Donuts* – so let's interrupt your walk to the station:

A young man, holding his head in muted exasperation. He's standing by his car – it's his, look at his stance, this is something he's *worked* for – and considering his options. The young man reaches down, and that's when you see the traffic cone caught between the wheel and chassis like a tight pinch. They lined the road, an inanimate sentry, protecting newly exposed trees, or no, the other way around, protecting pedestrian and vehicle from fallen arms. His own arms strain as he pulls at the plastic warbled by whatever collision took place here. You approach as his bunched fist swings at the orange cone, not disturbing that which has settled.

'I didn't see it,' he says. You don't remember him lighting a cigarette but it glows between his fingers. He blows air into his cheeks and stubs the small fire. He reaches down. You realize he has given up because he is being presented with no real choice at all. The traffic cone will not budge.

'You on your way to work?'

'Interview,' he says.

'Train?'

'I'll be late.' He checks his watch. 'Already running late. Shit, man.' The sigh he gives is tired. There is something here you recognize, knowing it so well yourself.

'Lemme get you an Uber,' you say, pulling out your phone.

'What? No –'

'I got you, man.'

'I couldn't. It's fine, I'll work something out.'

'Just get me back when you can.'

When you and he see each other next, you're walking home. He's going elsewhere. When he catches your gaze, his face splits open with joy.

'How you doing, man?'

'Can't complain, can't complain. You?'

'All good. Just on the way home.' He inhales from his joint and nudges you, a kind offering. You take the small fire from his palm, and puff, puff, your eyes crackling red with each soft gulp. Your pupils wide and black. Tired grin on his face. Headphones spilling sound into the night.

'What you listening to?'

'Dizzee Rascal.'

'Classic.'

'Seminal. No Dizzee, no me.'

You smile to yourself. A feeling nags at you that you cannot ignore.

'Can I take your photo?'

He looks surprised. It is one thing to be looked at, and another to be seen. You're asking to see him. He nods. You pull out the camera from your bag and train the lens on him. His eyes aglow, stealing what light remains in the sky. The slight smile on a kind face. You click on the shutter and his face opens in the moment the camera gasps. An honest meeting between two people. The gaze doesn't require words.

Walking on, you recall when you first heard the album, on a coach journey, on the way to Bournemouth. Martial arts was a way of trying to instil discipline in those searching for freedom. You lost the fight at the tournament that day but you felt brave regardless.

You were so surprised, hearing that big beat. Kick kick-snare, kick-kick, snare. Torn from elsewhere and stitched by hand into the fragment of the sparse garment. Wore the beat like a hat, soft on your head as your neck jerked back and forth with every snare, kick kick-snare, kick-kick, snare. The calls of Lon-don! Staying true to his grammar, to your grammar; brusque and utterly familiar. It was like hearing a friend's older brother telling tall tales you know to be true. The voice was utterly familiar: family friend, maybe, cousin – not blood, but no less so. *Fix up, look sharp*, the voice said. Had to switch it off after that track – the protests from the adults and parents – but the rush of hearing a forbidden truth, one steeped in your own truth, would not ease.

Richard, the owner of the cassette, was cool and never looked at you, but you knew he could see you. A pair of heavy gold medals swung from his neck. Earlier, you had all watched as he'd pivoted on the ball of his foot, swinging a vicious kick into the chest of his frightened opponent. He – the opposition – kept glancing towards his coach, wondering when the onslaught would stop. When Richard swept the first contender out of the ring, he stood facing another, four years his senior. Arms raised, Richard's stance easy, he launched a flurry of precise strikes, battering him with equal ease. You hovered round him, until he reached through his entourage towards you.

'What's up, little man?'

'Can you make a copy of that for me?' you asked, the young man towering over you. 'The tape?'

'You haven't heard it yet?'

He was so surprised when you shook your head, he handed you the tape in its case, Dizzee Rascal's *Boy in Da Corner* etched on the spine.

29

Let's go further back, to an early memory. 2001. In a living room which isn't your own, on a carpet worn down by shuffling feet and ashy knees. You've been running around ends with friends all day, and still you're stretching out these moments of carefree like they could be your last.

Flicking through TV channels, settling on MTV Base. The cackle of sped-up laughter, the question coming: 'What you laughing at?' A pair of children playing in wasteland. A flash of light and one transforms into a grown man, complete with bowler hat and round dark spectacles. All Black. They're all Black.

The second MC wears a leather durag atop his skull, a soft grin on the edge of his lips as he plays rapper for a few moments. Years later, you'll see him in a supermarket car park, his child slumped on his shoulder, still struggling to hold the boyish smile from taking over his features.

Now, forwards. Summer of 2016. You lost yourself in the mosh pit. Five pairs of hands – you could feel the purchase of each finger on your skin – pulled you back to your feet. Skepta ran out wearing shorts and thick black shades and a presence which filled the stage. That summer you'd been thinking about energy and frequencies, and how something could just feel right. When the DJ reloaded the posse cut for the third time, and five Black bodies moved freely across the stage, you thought, this feels right. This feels right.

Same summer. You're in Spain, on a beach where, on a clear day, you can see the shores of Morocco, when Frank Ocean's album,

Blonde, drops from the sky. This is not a drill. You've been waiting for something you didn't know you needed. When it comes, you take a pair of headphones, a folding beach seat, and stumble down the sand, watching the tide roll in and out. You can't remember knowing a stillness like this, and perhaps it's now, caught between looking forwards and looking back, you realize you're looking for it once more.

The sun rises late in this part of the world, and you watch as stars are replaced by a sheet of pale blue, a hot white dot climbing the sky. You didn't bring swimwear, so when you have finished listening to the album, you take off your clothes, and run into the water. Submerging, all you can hear is the rush, the roar. The salt of the sea mingling with your tears.

Forwards, once more. Six months ago. A slim figure, puffed by layers. Head bowed. All the candles have gone out, but he's illuminated by the darkness. It's the early hours of the morning. He's motionless, dancing to the sound of silence. The memorial is fresh. You wonder if the slim figure is also crying, like the moment you slid the key into the door, and broke down, unable to get the image out of your head: a bike lying on its side, the wheels still spinning back and forth, waiting for the rider to return. You wonder if he too is mourning Daniel, the kind man who won't ever get you back. That man who you shared a spliff with on roads and waxed into the night about Dizzee Rascal and grime and rhythm. That man who, for a moment, you loved like kin.

That afternoon: black and white uniform, deciding to show face. The station's just down the road, but you'll never find them in this place. Not unless something has happened. They go from shop to shop, off-licence, dry cleaner's, chippy, takeaway. They stop people in the street to ask for information. When they approach you, they stare, and remain silent.

The Caribbean takeaway doesn't have any patties, so you keep walking, onto the next one.

'How you doing, darling?' the woman behind the counter asks. You smile at how something as simple as a familiar inflection could cradle you in this moment.

Leaving, you hear a kick-kick, snare, kick-kick, snare in your ears. You wonder if Dilla added reverb to the snare, or cut it, clean, straight from a sample.

The interest in energies and frequencies remains, and you've always wanted to make music, always wanted to know whether you, too, could feel *just right*. Your friend, a drummer, invites you down to the coast and you record a music demo in a studio by the sea. The first take is fluffed, but you dance across the second, shoulders loose, punching words across the 64-bar count. You produced the beat yourself, so you know where the breaks lie, where the beat drags, where it slides, you're not surprised by the silence which you value so.

You gaze at the reflection of yourself in the glass of the booth, relaxed, unhurried, playing rapper for a few moments. You wonder if this is what freedom looks like.

You've been wondering about your own relationship to open water. You've been wondering about the trauma and how it always finds its way to the surface, floating in the ocean. You've been wondering about how to protect that trauma from consumption. You've been wondering about departing, about being elsewhere.

You have always thought if you opened your mouth in open water you would drown, but if you didn't open your mouth you would suffocate. So here you are, drowning.

You came here to ask for forgiveness. You came here to tell her you are sorry that you wouldn't let her hold you in this open water. You came here to tell her the truth.

30

She says:

She's been listening to rain fall at night. This is when she tends to pray, trying to manifest her desires in her own reality. Beside her bed, kneeling, never gazing skywards but into the ground, into the depths, wondering what lies beneath her surface. Her voice has grown loud in the quiet noise of her own thoughts. She's been thinking about you, and what you gave to each other. She's been thinking about loving you and what that meant. Your hearts were joined, beating in unison, but then they fractured, blood pooling and spilling in the darkness, and then they broke and that was that really. She still thinks about you a lot. Your lives unstitched themselves, but the loose threads remain where the garment was torn.

Under what conditions does unconditional love break? She cried for you yesterday. She has decided to submit to her tears rather than understand them. It's been a year at this point, but she knows she will always cry for you.

The thing that undid her was the memory of being seen. Do you remember? In the barbershop. She was in the chair. She remembers her presence changing the dynamic in the room; the presence of a woman in this masculine space meant everyone was either on their best behaviour or acting out. But in the moment she's referring to, quiet fell. You were watching her in the mirror, and she was gazing back at you. The barber cut the power of his clippers, to address you and her, to try to describe what he had seen pass between you, to let you know he saw you both. His excited chatter brought on smiles all round, nods of agreement. What more was there to say?

Language fails us, always. You told her that words were flimsy, so it was funny when you chose to write this. But she's grateful that you were able to give her this honest reality of yours. Lately, she's been thinking of other ways to say what cannot be rendered in language. She bought a camera, one like yours, an old 35mm. She has always wanted to take photos; there was a photo she saw at an exhibition which helped her make the jump: Roy DeCarava's *Couple Dancing, 1956*. The woman is wearing a white dress, the man a dark suit. Their figures emerge from the darkness, light catching hold of their limbs. They are pressed close, rhythm captured in the stillness. She saw you and her in that photo, in the glint of light on the woman's cheeks, in the man's arm clasped around the woman's back. In the trust and love being portrayed where light and dark were coexisting. And it's now she understands what you meant when you said the bulk of the camera felt heavier in your hands than it should. Seeing people is no small task.

She'd like to return to a memory of the present: you're both sitting on the hill in the park. It's been a year and your face is unchanged. Golden hour has come and gone, blue hour in its place, swathing you both in the soft hue of possibility. She begins to shiver and you offer your jacket, draping it over her shoulders. You're both enjoying the comfort of each other's silence. What more is there to say? She glances towards you and pulls her camera out of her bag. You joked as a photographer that you spent time chasing light, but you should've also said you bent darkness as well. She trains her lens on you and holds her breath before depressing the shutter. When the photo is developed, she's sure, if you look closely, you'll see the shadows cast across your skin, the eyes both seeing her and seeing the world, the honesty resting calmly on your features. If you look closely, you might see a tear making a journey from eye to cheek, as you cry for her. If you look closely, you'll see what she has always seen, what she always will: you.

Acknowledgements

To Seren Adams, I'll always remember our first meeting, where *Open Water* began. Thank you for all the support, editorial and otherwise, through the process. You're the best agent a writer could ask for, and a wonderful friend.

To my editors, Isabel Wall and Katie Raissian, thank you for taking so much time and care and affording this novel such a deep sensitivity. I'm beyond grateful.

To the team at Viking Books, thank you for working so hard to make this happen.

To my writing people: Belinda Zhawi, Candice Carty-Williams, Raymond Antrobus, Yomi Ṣode, Sumia Jaama, Victoria Adukwei Bulley, Kareem Parkins-Brown, Amina Jama, Joanna Glen – your words of advice and encouragement really got me over the line. Thank you.

To the homies: Krys Osei, Deborah Bankole, Rob Eddon, Stuart Ruel, Niamh Fitzmaurice, Justin Marosa, Courage Khumalo, Sam Akinwumi, Thomas McGregor, Charlotte Scholten, Nick Ajagbe, Alex Lane, Ife Morgan, Archie Forster, Louise Jesi, Chase Edwards, MK Alexis, Dave Alexis, Nicos Spencer, Law Olaniyi, Natasha Rachael Sidhu, Steffan Davies, Lex Guelas, Chrisia Borda, Mariam Moalin, Monica Arevalo, Luani Vaz, Charlie Glen, Diderik Ypma, Krystine Atti, Zoë Heimann and Cara Baker.

To Sue, thank you for always making me feel welcome and loved.

To Jashel and Jumal, thank you for always believing in me, and for pulling me up when my faith waned.

To Mum and Dad, I know how much you sacrificed in order for me to get to where I am now. I love you both, so much.

To Grandma, I know you're still smiling and singing for me.

Es, there aren't the words, but I won't stop trying.